T0147318

My Sxy Lil' Secrets

SxyChastity

AuthorHouse™
1663 Liberty Drive
Bloomington, IN 47403
www.authorhouse.com
Phone: 1-800-839-8640

First published by AuthorHouse 2/8/2011

ISBN: 978-1-4567-3393-3 (e)
ISBN: 978-1-4567-3392-6 (sc)

Library of Congress Control Number: 2011902206

Printed in the United States of America

A Military Thing

Today

A new day has begun, in the same bed, same house, same little town, but yet everything seems so different. Today, my priorities have totally changed. What a difference a day makes. Yesterday I was feeling just like every other day, like I didn't make a difference, like I was just another person without consequence in this big world, but then, I met you for the second time a few days ago. Our first meeting was in a faraway place, we were surrounded by thousands of people and yet we felt all alone, we were totally different people back then. You as always quiet and reserved, I always thought you just didn't like me, because you were never very friendly toward me but to this day I've never mentioned that to you, but since meeting again, everything is so different from that time long ago.

2003

We were deploying to Kuwait, the whole Battalion was on our way out, leaving our families, friends, loved ones, behind, not knowing for how long or if we'd ever see them again. My unit was tight, we'd been together for many years, and it was like family. But if you weren't among us, you'd never know how it feels to take people you love to a place of war, maybe you'd be losing them or vice versa them losing you. Many married, single, or like myself, single parents. Our families didn't know if they wanted to be proud, angry, sad, or just plain scared, that's the exact same way we felt. Every time one of us hugged our children or parent or spouse, it was so difficult to let them go. It was a very hard time for us, but we had each other.

I saw you from afar, My Sgt, I asked a mutual friend about you, she was kind of surprised of my interest in you, her words were, "hmmm interesting, he's not even your type." Funny, because I never thought I was a woman with a type, now, I know better. But anyways, we were in different units and not much time spent on the same bases. Yet still, the time I did see you, I was invisible in your eyes, not even a kind word in my direction. But like I said before, I now know this is you, my quiet soldier. We spent a year out there, being lonely, your mind going crazy thinking of the many things and problems going on in your house while you were out there in that damn war.

My agony was because of my children, their fathers not a part of their lives, and then me, the only person they have, so far away. My biggest fear while I was there was Michael's dad trying to take him away from me, my oldest, my sweet Michael. He wanted so much to act like a man, while being only 11. He didn't cry when I left, while I in turn couldn't stop. One whole year in a custody battle against a man that didn't even know him, no one knows my children like me. Maybe I'm not always the best mother, but I try so hard to give them everything they need and want. And the only way I was getting that done was being where I was, very far away.

Alex is so different from Michael; they are my day & night. Alex is emotional, but reserved. My baby, which is bigger than his older brother, so intelligent and yet so naïve, he is truthfully his age, just 9, when I left, he cried almost every night, because he thought I wouldn't be coming back. Then the one adult that I love more than anyone in the world becomes ill, I get back to my homeland to find her already operated on, I felt so helpless. What can I do? Except pray, I know I don't it do as much as I should, but at that moment I did. I had to go back before she was fully recovered, but thank God, she has a big family, and everybody chipped in to help take care of her and my children.

I have no idea what was going thru your mind, but we really didn't see much of each other, so I only thought of you, whenever I saw you, which wasn't very often. I made my time in the sand go by as fast as possible anyway I could, be it, going to the gym hours at a time, taking college courses, having brief affairs with other soldiers, which nothing came of them, and that was only the first few months there. I thank God so much for the few, sincere friends he put in my path while there. My friend Doris, who would stay up with me, till whatever time needed, while I waited for those terrible calls to let me know about the current custody of my Michael. Thank you so much for that, without you, I would've gone crazy. Girl you were the one person to keep me sane, you prayed for me and mine, so many times. You were my Angel in the Sand. And my other girl Rod, we would fight A LOT, but we would always make nice afterwards. Became friends after meeting on our first activation, you were going thru that nasty divorce, which in my mind was for the best. You kept me straight out there. And Alex's godmother, Brenda, my strength all the way back home. You would write and I would call, just keeping in touch, was enough to keep me sane.

At that moment in time I thought I was in love with the father of my youngest son, we had been together for about 11 years, and really not very good years, but when you believe that's who you love, that you can't do any better than that person or you just don't want to have to start all over again. I wasn't faithful to him, but why should I be, he was living with another woman, the one he left me for and had a child with, and yet, I still thought I loved him. How stupid can we, women be.

2004

I'm back home. I'm such different person. Everybody says so. I'm cold towards my children, even Alex's dad. I don't love anymore, well I do love my kids, but I'm not used to them near me anymore. Men wise, I guess just sex is good enough for now. Men only want what they can get from you, so why not we do it too? I mean what else do I need from a man, I have my own home, a car which is also mine, my children are well cared for. At this moment in time all I need is companionship and sex from a man, if indeed I'd find a man that is willing to be my one and only, I would definitely think about it. After many months back, I finally decide it's time to finish whatever I have with Alex' dad. I think he was expecting it, or maybe he wanted it over all along but was too much of a coward to do it himself. I will say, he wasn't stupid. He knew I did a lot for him, so why finish having a maid at your feet for free, someone who buys you clothes when you need it, cooks for you and gives you mind blowing sex whenever and wherever you want it. Who would let go of that intentionally? Well I had to finish it, I couldn't handle it any longer, being with a man I didn't trust. I wouldn't kiss him anymore, or even give him oral sex, never knew where his lips or dick were before me. How could I stay with a man like that? Who wouldn't respect me for the great woman I am, as the mother of his son. So I decided right before Christmas, that I value myself much more than he ever would, so I'd rather be alone with my sons, than with him. I cried for about 2 months, I wouldn't take his calls, at least not until I could take it, being alone again after so long, but in truth, I'd been alone for a long time already. I would not sleep in my bed any longer since I couldn't be alone in it, I hate being in my bed without the warmth of a male body. But I keep thinking that only good can come of this, maybe everything is for the better. Could it be that at last I'm ready for the man of my life to appear?

2008

Well I guess I was wrong. Here I am years later, still single. Having my fun, but nothing serious. Like I said before, if men can use us only for sex, why can't we use them? And at the moment, that's just what I'm doing. But since I saw you again, you reign my thoughts. Everyday has to begin with a thought of you, my day goes by thinking about how your day has been going?, had you eaten?, are you ok?, and when I go to bed, I wish your voice would be the last I hear before falling asleep and spend my night dreaming of you. After all I've been thru, how can I be so naïve, but yet I want to believe so much. Believe that you are the man that God sent for me, or maybe I was the woman to be yours all along, we were just in such a rush, or thought we were so in love with other people, that we missed each other by a few children and years. But at least I am ready to be where we are supposed to be, which I think is together. But always, a but, at this moment in time I don't think you are ready. Not ready for me, for a relationship, not even for love. I really do understand, not what you are going thru, but your state of mind. I just want you to know that I am here for whenever you need me. For whatever you need of me. I am yours for the taking, if you need a friend, I'm here. If you need a shoulder, here is mine. And love, if you ever need me to be your lover, I'm all yours. All you have to do is let me know and I will definitely make the time for you.

This is only a small part of all the things going on in my head, but

I do believe I had to start somewhere. Maybe next time I will tell you all about my childhood, or my relationship with my mother. Or better yet my love life, bet we have fun with that one.

Chastity 1

A Stranger

This is my fantasy.

In a hotel room that you have already paid upfront and in full. I am all alone waiting. Waiting for you. Room service knocks at the door, they said you wanted it to be served at this exact moment, champagne, wine, juices, cheese, strawberries, every type of melon (which by the way I love), bananas, the cart had a little bit of everything, to my surprise, another smaller cart rolls in, this one with whipped cream, chocolate syrup, Jell-O, cheesecake, chocolate cake, ice cream and bit and pieces more. I felt full just looking at all of it. I just left it all there and went to main suite to change.

I came out of the room and went straight to the balcony, beautiful view, the sun just about to set. I'm standing there in a short, sexy, almost see thru, red nightie, not caring who could see me, we were on the 7th floor, not too high not too low. I can already feel the dew in the breeze, feels like it's going to start raining soon. My nipples are getting hard, it's the breeze, the cold, the coming rain, but it's mostly anxiousness, I'm a bit nervous, because of you. Thinking of all we are about to do and the many things at our disposal to do so with.

Wait................. there's someone at the door, it must be you. But I don't turn to see. I just wait. I can hear you putting your keys on the table. I feel you just standing there, looking at me. I don't dare move, I feel as if you are physically touching me and yet you are still in another room, you move, towards me, closer. Until you are directly behind me, I still don't look, at that exact moment you whisper from behind telling me to close my eyes and just relax. I feel you so much closer but still not touching me. My hands get tighter on the railing, anticipation getting the best of me. At last I feel you, and realize that I'm not the only one excited about this meeting. You are so close, but we are quiet no one speaks, not a bad silence, but a calming one, just us and this spectacular view. You move your hands closer to my body, now on the railing on both sides of me.

You bend closer and just inhale the scent of my hair, nibble my earlobe, start kissing my neck and my shoulder, then you tell me how much you love how I smell and feel. Your hands grab my hips just to pull me closer to you, now I feel your body completely against mine, your erection pressing against my behind, you feel so big, so hard. I was about to turn around, but you stop me and again say, no looking just relax.

The rain begins, but only a little drizzle, not very much, it feels so cool against my hot skin, you ask me if I want to go inside, I say no. Might seem a bit corny, but I've always wanted to have a romantic interlude in the rain, it's what I want. You keep caressing, kissing, touching and I'm just taking it all in. Then you put your cheek to my wet hair and say how beautiful I am to you and that you love the way I feel all wet. I just sag against you; your hands are all over and yet so sensual. The sun is about to set and the sprinkling rain makes it all the more beautiful, at last I'm totally relaxed. But at that exact moment you take me by surprise, you bend me forward just a bit on the railing and impale me from behind, taking me so completely. Your hands on my hips, moving me to you, I feel the whole of you and it's just so great. Your hands move to my breasts and you are holding on tightly but lovingly, then I feel everything coming to me at once. I feel as if I'm about to free fall into a great dark hole, there's no railing, nothing to hold on to, just the fall, but then I feel you holding on so tight and we take the jump together. It's incredible!!

I just sag against your body and you don't disappoint me, You hold on to me like there's no tomorrow and still you ask me to keep my eyes closed. We are all wet, almost can't stand because of the grand orgasm and you ask me to keep my eyes closed. And I do as I'm told. It's all been so great. I don't even know how much time has passed since I got here and now. You take my hand and pull me inside, I hear the shower being turned on, I feel the steam of the hot water, and you take off the rest of my clothes and tell me to stand under the water so I can warm up after being in the rain for so long. I can see you are used to being in charge, because you are just so bossy.

After 10 minutes I call for you, no answer, I get out and find a note and 1 white rose on the pillow, it says, " My love, thank you for trusting me so with your body, I'm asking you now to trust me with your heart................ Can you? We will be together soon enough, but just so you know, this wasn't our 1st time and by all means it will not be our last.

Love you!
Me

This is just one part of my fantasy; we still have a couple of carts full of goodies.

Chastity 2

All Tied Up

You are so late, you know I just hate waiting, even for you, even though I really love the way you sex me, but making me wait, don't think so, you got 10 more minutes or I'm gone. At that exact moment my phone rings, a private number, lately that's how you've been calling with one excuse or another, you say, " Please don't leave I'm almost there, I have a surprise for you." I just straight out tell you, that you have 10 minutes or I'm out, I hang up and exactly 9 minutes later, I hear a car. I just lay in bed in my white camisole and hot pants. We know the type of relationship we have, not a lovey dovey one, but a very sexual one, we do caress, kiss and whisper sweet nothings, but we are clear it will never go beyond that. Am I a bitch for this? Oh well, that's how you like me. You walk in with a full bag and a cooler, I ask "what's all that?" You just tell me not to be so damn nosy, that I'll find out soon enough. We've talked about many sexual fantasies, both, yours and mines, but have always kept it straight, since we only see each other once or twice every couple of months, we are so hungry for each other we can't wait, and afterwards we are so exhausted or one of us is in a hurry to leave, that we haven't had the opportunity to embrace our fantasies.

You kiss me and wish me a happy birthday, I was amazed that you'd actually remember, because truthfully, I don't even know when yours is, to say the truth I don't even know your last name. Everything is put away, you come back to the bed and tell me how pretty I look for you and there we start our foreplay. Boy, today you are really in the mood, your hands are just everywhere, your mouth (God bless that mouth), you can drive me crazy just with your mouth. But you stop, you tell me to sit up, I do, expecting you to let me sit on your lap facing you and you do, but you get a silk handkerchief and tell me to close my eyes so you can put it on; what is it with men and closed eyes? But, I do never the lest. Never been blindfolded before, usually I'm the one in control, I feel so vulnerable, can't see anything. You lay me on my back and start caressing me again, go down to my legs, oh I know where you are going, but again you stop and start massaging my legs, only to tie them down also, you tell me to calm down, it will be all so good, this will be all for me, my birthday present. It doesn't seem like much of a present to me, since I'm the one all tied up here, but again I submit. Someone should come in and hit me over the head, for letting you do all this, since I don't even know your last name, but life has to end one way or another, how better than this. Call me crazy. Well getting back to my birthday present..............

You tie only one of my wrists, and just tell me I must have self control of my other hand and not touch you or myself at any moment. Do you know what you are asking of me? To not touch you!!! But I enjoy touching you, you are my aphrodisiac, licking, kissing and touching you makes me wet. How can you ask me not to? You tell me to behave and enjoy the ride. I'm on my back just waiting, I hear you walking around the room, sounds of opening packages and bottles, then silence. I could smell the black cherry candle I like so much. You kiss me, you taste of chocolate, I raise my head for more, you put a chocolate covered finger in my mouth, I suck it all off while listening to you moan. And I know we are both thinking about when I suck your delicious dick. You step away and say "my turn", I feel thick, warm liquid on my nipples, I think its chocolate but it seems thicker somehow, then my mind just focuses on your mouth, aggressively suckling on whatever you poured on my nipples, my free hand shoots out to grab your head and keep you to my breast. Big mistake. You pull away and tell me that for misbehaving, I'm getting a 3 minute time out. I'm like whatever, 3 minutes aren't shit. Boy was I wrong. You didn't talk or touch me at all, absolutely nothing, just the smell of the candle and now I can distinguish the smell of what you poured on me, I can almost bet its honey, plus I can still taste the chocolate in my mouth, on my tongue. I ask you, "What type of birthday present is this? When I'm the one being punished?" Still, no answer. I never knew how long 3 minutes really were. I'm getting kind of aggravated, but just then, your mouth is on my other nipple, the liquid is already quite hard, so you nibble, using your teeth, which is a big time turn on, since I've always liked it a bit rough, not too much but you know how much. You pull on my nipple with your teeth, it hurts, but I'm not about to complain. Your hand finds my pussy, which is already very wet, you finger me for a few seconds, just enough to get me more worked up and then you stop everything. I wait......... but have to open my mouth, "Where are you? I haven't touched you, why did you stop?" I feel you standing close to the bed, your hand caresses my belly, I shiver, you just tell me to be patient and let you take over and that if I complain again, I would have a 5 minute time out. You know I shut my big mouth.

As soon as I shut up, I felt something cold being poured on my stomach, when I flinched because of the cold surprise, I felt it going down to my pussy, you just said, "I'm so thirsty" and started licking and sucking my stomach, said you still needed more, poured some more straight on to my pussy and just licked slowly, started sucking on my lips and then I felt your tongue start going in and out, Mmmmm , I want to hold your head down to my pussy so bad, but I know better now, so I just bring my hips up to you, like I said before, you are a miracle worker with your mouth, just when I'm about to cum, you stop again. You tell me to open my mouth to you, so I do, there's a strange noise, then you put your finger in my mouth again, but this time covered in whip cream, you say enough, I hear the noise again, but now you are straddling me, I know what's to be in my mouth next. Your dick is now not just delicious but also sweet. You know to let me guide it into my mouth, no pushing it in or pulling my head, you can grab my hair and hold on. Today it's a bit tricky since I'm all tied up, but I manage, quite nicely if I say so myself, how great to hear you moaning my name, but papi, if it's my birthday and I'm not cumming, you for sure aren't going to cum yet. You get off without a word knowing I won't finish you off, just yet. You pour something else on me all the way from my kitty up to in between my tits, this feels weird, but it's also cool, you start slurping it all off, with a quite frenzy, not a word said, just your mouth on my body. Me, well you're driving me crazy, and your hands are not even touching me, just that glorious mouth and you haven't even reached my hot spots yet. When your mouth comes down on mine, Oh My!! You taste so sweet, you are between my spread legs, just kissing my mouth, neck and shoulders, then, in a flash, you are completely in me, I cum so fast, I can't believe it, you keep going and say now it's your turn. You bite down on my shoulder as you cum hard inside of me. As we are getting our breath back, I feel so damn sticky; I caress your face and ask to take everything off of me. As you do, you tell me how much more I opened up to you, since I couldn't see you looking, you told me how beautiful my body moves for you when there's no inhibitions. I blush, since I'm not used to you being so complimentary towards our sex. But after the ties are taken away and just the blindfold still on, you come close and whisper in my ear, "I want you for myself, I don't want anyone else kissing or touching your body, caressing your heart or loving your soul, only me, after tonight, please tell me it will only be me, answer me before the blindfold is off. If your answer is no, once I take off the blindfold, it will be as it's always been and the words I just said were all part of the fantasy, if you say yes, this will always be the special moment where we started a love story."

How was I to answer that? A single tear falls thru the blindfold and you kiss it away. Maybe this is what I've always wished for, you and me. Am I ready? You tell me.................................

Chastity 3

Just thinking

The day has been so hectic at work and yet every minute my mind has a chance to wander, it's you who I think of. Those few and sparse moments, in which I think of the way you know exactly how and where to caress me and at what exact moment. Sometimes it seems we are connected on some higher level, because you know when I need you, when I need that tight hug or just a simple kiss on the temple, but you are so in tune with me sexually, that you can feel when I'm not feeling sexy, when I feel like an ugly duckling. At that moment you tell me how beautiful and sensual I am to you. Maybe its fate, that we ended up together, but I thank God for you every day, just in case. You are truly my other half, maybe even my better half, since I still have a bit of wild running around. But thinking of you in those few minutes or even seconds makes my day a whole lot brighter. My coworkers are happy about us, because now I'm rarely in a bad mood anymore and that's all thanks to you.

Imagine how people will react when we tell them the funny story of how we really met, not even in person, but on the internet, looking at pictures of one another and believing whatever each of our profiles said about each other. We being far away from each other, so we could only call, e-mail and text, but that was enough at the moment, I was still flirting around here in Puerto Rico, God knows what you were doing in The States, come on I'm not naïve, but I liked very much what I was hearing and seeing from you, so why not give it a try. But you are such a complicated guy and yet simple, each day that went by I found myself thinking of you more and more. We made plans, well truthfully, you did, for you to come down to Puerto Rico for a few days and really get to know each other. You said you'd be here in July and then made me wait almost to the last moment to tell me exactly when you would be here, it was nerve wrenching, the wait, not knowing what to really expect, if you were going to like who I am, if I was going to like you.

You arrived just after my birthday and I was so happy to finally meet and spend time together. You were truly everything I had ever wished for and a bit more. Funny, romantic, caring and so sexual. There we got along very well. We had sex every day, morning, noon and night, and every moment we were alone we were kissing and touching, even when we were out and about, you let it be known I was with you and I liked that very much. I was so sad when the time for you to leave arrived. I didn't want you to go. I already missed you, your hands on my body, your mouth on mine, feeling you enter me as if you've always belonged there, as if I was made just for you. But you had to get on that plane and back to work.

We knew we wouldn't be seeing each other for a while because of my work, but a few months away after that whirlwind weekend, would let us think about what we want from each other, is it just sex or the real thing? I knew I wanted you forever in my life after that weekend, even during, I already knew, but it was going to be difficult since we are far from each other. It would be difficult for you to get a job that paid as good here and then I have everything in Puerto Rico, my job, my house, my family and most importantly my children. What are we gonna do? I still need you to vent on how it went for you and whatever your thoughts are on all this. So how about it? Are you the one I've been waiting for all this time or are you just another frog until I kiss the one that is my prince? I really hope you are it. I guess we'll see...............

Chastity 4

All About You

Well here I am still waiting on you, you said you'd be here, but I guess plans change when you least expect them to. Too bad, I guess, I really wanted to get to know you, meet you in person at last. Just hope that the meeting will come eventually and that this is as serious as you make it out to sound. But let me give you something to look forward to.

This is kind of what I had envisioned for our long weekend together:

First of all, by Thursday the kids would already be staying at their grandmothers, while I worked in the morning, anxious to get home and get ready to go pick you up at the airport. Primping, shaving everything, wash my hair and oil down my body so it's nice and smoother than usual. Get into something sexy that shows off my breasts and legs. At the airport, I'll be waiting right by the car or if you want I can wait at the arrival gate, so you can see how sexy other men think your girl is. I'll leave that to you, let me know. Well anyways, we've seen each other in pictures, so nothing shocking when we finally see one another; you grab me and kiss me right then and there, nice. Let them know I'm taken. We get to my car and there you sit me on the hood, stand between my legs and kiss me hard while your hands roam my body, I'm beginning to think you like what I have on. I tell you to give me a minute; my panties come off and there begins our first sexual encounter, a quickie on top of the hood of my car in the airport parking lot. It's good, but I want more and since I know we can't have it here, I decide it's time to head home. Great start to our weekend together don't you think? It's already kind of late, I ask if you want to stop for something to eat, but we're just not really hungry (for food that is), we stop at a supermarket to pick up some fruit and stuff like that.

I suggest we stay at a motel for the night, we're half way home, we agree to one with a Jacuzzi, since I don't have one at the house (Yet!!). Once we inside, it hits me, that I have you here at last, even though we already had a try, I feel a bit shy with you, well maybe shy is not the word, more to the point would be insecure, you are used to being around women with spectacular bodies and truthfully, mines needs a bit of work. I want to turn the lights off, you don't want to hear of it, and you tell me how much you want my body as is. We start undressing each other slowly, just taking everything in. your body is just perfect; love the tattoos, so damn sexy. I want to touch every inch, touch you all. We just caress each other for the longest and of course lots of kissing. Then I just get out of bed, take your hand and head towards the Jacuzzi. I love sex in the water, the only thing is, with you I hope it's more than just sex. We spend a little while just soaking in the water and rubbing each other, I want you so bad already. You grab me and sit me on the edge of the tub, but you stay in just pulling my legs apart and getting in between, you are so close to my pussy. I can feel your breath on her, but you just blow on her softly, Oh My! Your hands are soft on my thighs, then you grab my hips to pull me closer, at last I can feel your mouth on me, you are so tender, but then I grab your head to pull you closer and that was all you needed for you hunger to ignite, it felt like you'd been waiting for this all your life and I've been needing you all of mine. My orgasm came out of nowhere and everywhere, but that wouldn't be the end of it, since you decided you wanted to feel all of me at that moment, so you took what is yours, you were in me so fast, I didn't register. Still riding the first wave, you gave me what I wanted, All of you. You brought me back down into the water, it felt so great. You are sucking my breast, which makes me cum on itself (hint, hint); imagine that plus the feel of your hot, throbbing dick all in me. I had to let go. I thought I'd faint, it was so strong, but I had to hold on a bit longer for you, but that didn't take long after mine, you bit down on my shoulder when I felt your creamy, hot cum in me, Mmmmmm. We stay in the water just like that, me straddling you, face to face. We kiss and decide we should get at least a few hours of sleep; it's already about 2am on your first day on the Island. Hope you've liked your stay so far……..

I wake up and see it's almost 6am; we only got a couple of hours left here, since, for your information, motels in P.R. are only 8 hours a stay. I feel absolutely great, fabulous sex and to wake up in the arms of this utterly sexy man completes it. As much as I don't want to, I unwrap myself of you and head to the bathroom, as soon as I get thru with my business, I jump back into bed with you. Snuggle up close and at this moment take my time looking at your ink, you try to pull me closer and I just tell you to chill and let me look. I look, touch and kiss every piece of art on you, you are a piece of art. You tell me to give you a minute to take a shower and stuff; I just say hurry back I'm not done with you yet. You are done in a flash and jump right back into bed again. I know we don't have a lot of time left here so I do what I want to do, which is, take you in my hand, caress the whole of it and kiss the head. Baby are you ready? Well I've been for a while, I suck on just the head for a few and then start licking it all, you think I can get it all in? I'm surely going to try. After a few minutes you cum for me, nice, now get ready, we have to go.

We stop to have breakfast on the way and since we are close, I drive by Luquillo beach (my favorite), we get out of the car and sit on the sand for a while, just being there with you makes it all different, you grab and pull me so I am now sitting in between your legs and hold on to me from behind, feels so good to have you here, it's like a missing piece being found. I've spent only 1 night with you and it feels like we've been together forever. We spend the morning at the beach just chillin' and talking (which you don't do much), we touch but nothing mayor, we kiss a lot, but let's go home it's almost lunch time already. We hit a Chinese restaurant for takeout, we get home at last. I show you around, my place isn't big so it only takes us a minute, then we sit down to have lunch together. Afterwards you want to shower, so I get you a towel and show you the way, you suggest I shower to since we still have sand on us, I say later you say now, so we shower together, bathe each other. You are hard and ready for some more, I bend over and give you what you want, you take it hard, we are so slippery, you feel so smooth going in and out, and I want to feel you like this always. We finish up and take a well deserved nap (naked), since we really haven't slept much. A few hours later, I feel this heady sensation, I feel so wet, and then I know why. You are in between my legs again just going at it, guess you liked my kitty, I know I love that mouth. You notice me awake and maneuver a bit to bring that delicious dick up to me, nice way to wake up, 69 is great; I cum in your mouth while you cum in mine. We take a quick shower and head out to catch a movie. Decent movie, but I'm all into my company, I take your dick out right there, just so I can touch you, just love touching you, so we masturbate each other right there, wait for the movie to be over and then step into the rest rooms and get fixed up. We go to The Flamboyan in Luquillo for a bit of pool and a few drinks, some of my friends are waiting for us there to finally meet you, since most everyone has seen your picture. We stay for a couple of hours, then we all roll to Fajardo and check out Players and Sharkys, there I can really dance, that's until you say we should go home, cause you just want to fuck me silly after all that grinding against you all night, it's about 3am already anyways, so we say our goodbyes. We get home and even though I know how horny you are , our lovemaking (that's what it feels like this time) is slow and so tender, when we are done we fall asleep just as we are, you buried deep inside of me.................

Well it's Saturday morning already, half way thru your stay. Today is beach day, today you meet some of my family and most importantly my children, it'll be a fun day. I make you breakfast and get you out of bed; I'm already done, just waiting on you, babe. We're off at about 10am, stop and buy some beers, sodas and munchies. We get there and my cousin is already there, chairs out, cold beer, just waiting, it's such a beautiful day. We get to jump in the water alone for a little while before everybody else gets there; once they arrive the craziness begins. All the kids, everybody talking at the same time, English, Spanish, back and forth. Well the females in the family agree I've done well with the sexy Porto Rican who thinks he's a white boy in my life, things seem good. We go back in the water and you pull me into your arms, I bring you into a hug wrapping my legs around you, you slide my bikini bottom to the side and finger me for a while, but I want you in me, so you oblige and give me what's mine, slowly and carefully since there are so many people and they might notice what we are up to, the adults, I could care less if they know or not, but the kids I do. You kiss me while you cum in my throbbing pussy. You are just going to drive me insane before you leave. We wait a bit and then get out and socialize over some bar bq hot dogs and beers, we start out home at about 6pm. I'm so tired, I jump in the shower (ALONE), because if not we won't get out. Tonight we staying home watching a movie or two. After you take a shower, you lay in my lap while we watch the first movie, not even 30 minutes into the movie you're out for the count. I don't care, I like being able to just caress and look at you like this. When the movie is over, I wake you up to go to bed, where we cuddle and both fall asleep.

Well it's Sunday, we make it a late morning, have quiet morning sex, I love spooning in the morning. Today I'm taking you to the Bacardi factory, take the tour, have some drinks, get some souvenirs for you to take back. Today we're having an early dinner at my ex in-law's home, she wants to meet you. See it's not every day that I have someone staying at my house, which I consider special, so everyone is just curious about you. We get there pleasantries are made, we have dinner and coffee, and out the door we go. We get home by 8pm. I let you know I want to spend our last night together just enjoying each other, no TV, no more going out, no friends, just you and I. We take a long shower together and then go to bed naked, a lot of kissing, talking, touching and we spent most of the night making love one way or another, it's fun but sad, I will miss having you in my bed and in my life here so much. We get up at about 9:30am, jump in the shower, have some coffee or juice and get dressed. Start getting your stuff ready; put it in the car so we don't have to come back to the house to pick it up later. We go by my grandma's house for lunch and goodbyes, everything goes nicely. Time to go since your flight is early evening, don't want to be late. On the way we talk about me going to you, a lot of planning since I start school soon, but it definitely will happen. We hold hands and kiss a lot, but you have to go now. Have a great trip and don't forget about me now..................

Hope this sounds like fun; it's just an incentive for you to come and spend time with your girl. Maybe not exactly how it's written but along those lines is what I wanted for us. Sorry I missed the hammock part, but that you will have to come and find out. Expect to see you soon.....................

Much Love,
Your Girl,
Sandy

Chastity 5

Three's Enough

When we first got together, we spoke out each other's fantasies, things we wanted to do to each other and we hadn't done with anybody else. After being a couple for a few months, most of our fantasies were already reality. Like tying each other up, integrating food in sexual intercourse, sex in very public places, role playing by each of us, but we still have a few to go, since it was a long list once we put both together. But the one I knew you really wanted, but didn't push for, because now we were serious about each other, and that little fantasy was the threesome. I really didn't like the idea of sharing you or being shared by you, but I believe a woman should satisfy her man's needs or somebody else will do the job for you. And let me tell you, sexually, I can get as down and dirty as the busiest street corner hoar. But even though, this was a big step, a lot of trust goes into this type of situation, so I came up with a plan:

We will do this once and only once, it'll be 2 girls, this including myself and you, most importantly, I pick the girl (which I already have in mind) and you will not see her at any moment, hear her voice or know her name, because you would be blindfolded the whole time. These are my rules, now it's up to you to take it or leave it and just know it's a onetime offer, never again will you get the opportunity if you turn it down now. You think it over, I believe more for my benefit than yours, since you know deep down I don't want this and it would be all for you. But being a man given your fantasy on a silver platter, you grab it with both hands; you accept and just ask, when? Well it will take a few weeks since I have to convince my girl Lyn (not her name) and plan babysitting, because it would be at the house.

Why Lyn you ask? Well we kind of did something like this before, but with her man and there was no sexual intercourse involved, just a lot of kissing, touching and dick sucking. It was wild, maybe I'll tell you about it someday soon. But, that is the reason I trust and want it to be Lyn. At no moment will my man know her name or who it is. Why is this so important to me? Well like I said, she is my friend, so maybe at one moment in time or another, we all go out together or she and her family come by the house or we to theirs and I don't want him getting ideas. But let's get down to your fantasy.

It's a Saturday night, kids are at grandmas, the house is nice and quiet, no TV, no lights, only lots of candles and nice, slow music. We're snacking on some fruit and wine, it's almost time, I told Lyn 11pm, so most my neighbors were either asleep or out. I'm nervous, only been thinking about how all this is gonna go. Will you like being with her more than me? Will she suck you off better? Will you enjoy her pussy and her touch more than mine? These are the questions on the minds of every woman that does this for her man. I just hope we never regret this. Well its 10:45, time to stop thinking and start acting. I straddle you and feel you immediately get hard, one of the many reasons I love you, I kiss you and say let's go to the bedroom. Once there, the ambience is already sexy, smells like mint and vanilla, a few candles here and there, air conditioner is going, everything is ready. Are you? Well ready or not here we go. "Baby close your eyes, first I'm putting a black silk handkerchief, and then a black bandana, making sure you can't see anything. Let me help you lay back, quick kiss and I'll be right back." My girl, on time as usual, I let her in, we have a glass of wine together while you wait in the room, we're talking strategy and how much fun it will be. I really hope so. I let her know she can't speak, everything will be done by eye contact, signs and touching, she has no problem with that, so hand in hand we head for my room, as I open the door you jump a bit in response. We look at you appreciatively from afar. Only have on the handkerchief and the silk boxers, nice. We nod at each other and it begins.

Each one at either side of you, we start touching you, our hands touching the same part of your body at each side at the same time, you tremble. You turn to me asking for a kiss, you say you know my touch, that really makes me happy, I grab your face and we both start at your earlobes, then your neck, cheeks and start kissing you simultaneously, a little her, a little me. We can see how excited you are, your dick is hard and straight up and we still haven't even gone there. We move off the bed and take off our panties, grab your boxers and pull them off slowly with our teeth, you can feel our breath on you, all the way from your waist down to your legs, as soon as it comes off, and we can see the precum, shiny on the tip of your beautiful, big, hard cock. We start kissing your calves, knees, thighs and then to the prize, we both start licking, kissing and sucking you, head, core, testicles, everything, you grab both our heads, you're trembling. We stop a moment, but just to put a condom on you, then we both straddle you, one on your face and the other on your dick, we are facing away from each other, after a good while we start switching around, putting tits in your mouth, your dick between some tits, sucking you all over. You had us both on your mouth, on your dick and your hands were greedily all over our bodies. Your mouth was always too busy to say anything. We did it doggy style, while the other girl was getting her pussy eaten, then we switched and you got some ass, while sucking tits and kissing hard. We all had cum a few good times, so Lyn and I look at each other and smile, guess this was it. She kisses you; I kiss you and tell you to stay still. We girls leave the room, I get a beer and towel for each of us, she gets in the shower, I sit on toilet seat and we talk and laugh, in whispers, since the room is nearby. We know this is a onetime thing (at least with my man). Then I get in the shower while she dresses, when I finish, I bid her farewell, thank her and let her know we will talk later on. I walk back into the room 30 minutes later, this time you stay still, looks like you fell asleep, I just stand there looking at you, naked and blindfolded, and you are so beautiful. I lay next to you, loving the smell of you, I touch your shoulder, right where you have that tattoo I love (I really love all your tattoos), still sweaty, but I don't care, I kiss you and then I know you are not asleep when your hand slides up my body to grab a fistful of my hair. You ask if you can finally take off the blindfold, I say of course. You whip it off, give me a quick kiss and jump off the bed, you say you need a shower and a beer with your girl, I tell you I'll get the beer while you're in the shower, but you stop me and say, "I said I need a shower and a beer WITH my girl, that means you and I in the shower, understood." I thought you might want some time alone to think about all that happened tonight. But you just want me, a lot had to do with doing this all for you and me letting you know how much I trusted you and loved you and you didn't need any more time thinking about it. It happened, we all had fun and now the fantasy is over and my reality is a lot better. I gave my man the fantasy of every man and he took it, enjoyed it and came back to me completely and happy. Now my reality is loving this man I have the best I can, now that the biggest fear (fantasy) is done and over, we can see about the next step or maybe even the next hot fantasy............

Chastity 6

Unattached

Well here I am again, and let me assure you that everything you read with my name on it, has happened, will happen or I've dreamed it all up. You think you can figure out which is fact and which is fiction?

This time I'm just gonna go to being unattached, this is one thing men can do really well, but we girls have a hard time at. For them sex is just sex, they can go ahead and have an affair and go back home, get found out and say, "Baby it was just sex, I love you." What kinda shit is that? But most of the time we forgive you buttheads. What if it were the other way around? Easy. You would just kick us to the curve and say, "Next". But guess what? Times have changed. Double standards no more. Let me tell you a little story...........

When I was in my mid twenties, I separated from my baby's daddy; it was a bad time, real bad time. It had been only him for the longest, so I would cry all the time, be in shitty moods, take it out on everybody, just be in pissy fit mode all day, every day, until I just let it all out and figured out a way to deal with it better. And the best way to do that is having sex and me being an attractive, sexy, young thing, didn't have a problem getting men interested in a "sex only" kind of thing, not a problem at all.

I was working on base (Rosey Rds); I had a variety to pick from, Army, Air Force, Navy, Marines, Coast Guards, Special Forces, FBI, DEA, every armed forces and federal agency services. WOW! Let me tell you how it all started, the day I found my man with his mistress, I went on a drinking spree with who was then my best friend, where did we go? On base. So you know MP's were watching us drink up a storm, so when we left, so did they. We swerved once and not even because we were drunk, it was putting in a damn cd, they turned on the lights, I said keep going no sirens, but once we got to the gate, we had four patrol cars waiting for us, so we had to stop. Patrolman T, walked up to us, sexy black man, but I was too drunk to be interested, my girl was tipsy but good, T talked a lot of blasé, blasé, bullshit, bullshit. I just said give us the damn ticket so we can go to sleep. T was pissed but ask me if I care. Then he looked me over and asked if I worked in a nearby restaurant, I said, "Well not that it is any of your business, but yes." He smiled and said, "You're a little bitch and I like that, no ticket this time." What?! All these patrol cars and no ticket, my girl just sped off. A few days later he walks into my place of business, all smiles. I treat him with a bit of indifference, but now sober, notice how sexy he is. He's over there trying to make jokes about pulling me over, I'm not laughing. When T is about to walk out with his food, he turns back, gives me a paper with his name and number, tells me to please call me and that his given name is Travis. I do call but after a few days that is. We meet and there begins my affair with Travis.

That first phone call, we made everything clear, all cards on the table, we were going to initiate an open sexual relationship, no bf-gf kinda thing, no jealousy fits, just regular booty-calls, and he was to be my main go to man and I, his main sex kitten. Nice arrangement, since we could both sex outside our nest. But let me tell you people something; this man wasn't the most attractive man of them all, not even tall, about 5'7", but the sexiest of them all, booming body, bedroom eyes, soft brown skin and literally the best sex I've ever had in my whole life and that says a lot.

The first time we were together, we just went wild on each other, it felt so releasing. When I finally got home, I felt like I had been in a marathon, all my muscles ached, but it was a good pain. After that we would see each other a few times a week and it was always good, he would call me or I him, it didn't matter, we made it happen. It would always be at his place since I had the kids, was more comfortable and a lot simpler. Our little affair had been going on for about 5 months when T started telling me that his roommate was interested in me and that he (T) didn't have a problem sharing. See even though we were open like that, I respected T enough not to look at his boy like that, I had noticed him, I mean who wouldn't? The guy played football, nice body, beautiful smile, tall, dark and very handsome. But even with all that going for him, we never even spoke much, only hi or bye, if he opened the door for me when I went to fuck T or if he came by my job. I just told T that his boy could look all he wanted but I wasn't gonna go there. But my sexy T was very insistent on it. Most of the times I went to see him he had one comment or another that he said his roomie (Chris) had said, like how much he liked my tits or my skin color, or even that I had the most beautiful legs he had seen, T would say some outrageous things, but I just left everything as was for the time being.

One day in Oct, T called me for sex and once I got there we stayed in the living room, something strange since we went directly to his room every time and we never really talked or watched TV, we would get together and straight out fuck and I would bounce. But that particular day, T and C were watching football together, and if you know me personally, you know I love football (except college ball). So I walk in and say hi to C, give T a kiss and sit my pretty ass down to watch the game with them. 15 minutes later T gets a call and tells me he has to go to his job on base, but that it will only take him at most half hour and he'd be back, so I'm about to jet, but T tells me to please wait for him there at this crib since he won't be long and he still wants to sex me, and if you ever had sex with T, you really wouldn't want to miss out on that. I asked C if it wouldn't bother him if I stayed and finished watching the game with him, he said no problem. T leaves. Chris and I, alone in the house for the very first time, we just watched the game in silence for a good 15 minutes, then I start talking, you know how your nerves get when you are in a place all by yourself with a very sexy man, 2 beds and a sofa available? Well that was definitely me and since T had put all those thoughts of C saying things about me in my head, my thoughts were going wild at the moment. I just asked what team he was rooting for, he said the opposite of mine, so it was on; we started fighting over any flag thrown out, over every pass and touchdown. But then I had to go get physical, I poked him in the ribs saying my team was going to win, he poked back, then we started tickling each other, until he fell off the sofa, there he was right in between my legs, staring into my eyes, so close, I had to, I gave him a peck and everything got serious. I said I was sorry, since I started it all. C didn't move from where he was, but did make a bit of space between us. He said nothing like that should ever happen again because I was seeing T, at that moment I had to explain to him about the arrangement T and I had. I asked him if he didn't want anything with me then why he was telling T things about me, as in complimenting my body and the type of woman I was. He just stared at me and said, "T told me you were asking about me and saying how you wouldn't mind getting with me." Now we just stare at each other like, what the hell is going on here? We talk it out for about an hour and you come to the conclusion, that the only logical reason for all this is that T wants a threesome and what better way than to get your best friend and the girl you are fucking together to make it happen. I tell C straight out, I'm not down for no threesome, but then he asks me if something can still go on between us. I just think we need to back away slowly from all of this and see what happens. But we do exchange cell phone numbers (since I already know your home number, jajaja) and kiss some more. 2 or 3 hours had gone by and T hadn't made it back yet, I leave, because temptation like C is not a joke. Called T, he said we'd talk in person the next day. C called and we spoke all night long. Next day, I went to the crib to ask T some questions, he said exactly what C thought he would, he wanted a threesome with me and his best friend, I said no. He said not to jump the gun and have sex with C, then give him an answer, then he threw me on the bed, took off my clothes and fucked me royally. He said just thinking about it got him hard, so we fucked a good 2 hours and since C was at work it was all good. That was until C called later that afternoon and asked why I had fucked T, and I told him, he knew I was still with T and that's what we do, just unattached good sex. And really, I don't know what C's problem is, he had a girlfriend. Well that's men for you, they can get theirs and we gotta lie about it, well that's not about to happen here. This is how it all began sexually with Chris........

C called and asked me to come by the house, I asked him if T was there, he said no. So I went. We talked and watched a movie, and then we went into his room, where we took everything nice and slow. C was so patient and caring, while I just wanted to rip his clothes off. I hate comparing, but it was so different than my times with T. I can't compare, since T is rough and wild and still the best sex ever, as where C is slow and sensual, even a bit romantic I'd say. Now I really can say that I am enjoying the best of both worlds, I am eating my cake and my ice cream too. The next day I sat them both down and set ground rules: First, I would not sex one if the other is in the house. Second, no jealousy trips by either of them. Third and not least, no talking to each other about encounters with me. Am I good or what? The best part of it all, they both agreed, so here it is as it stands, T and I are in a very open relationship, but no one serious on the sides. And then C and I, well he has his girlfriend and me, no one else and I do as I please. Nice plan, huh?

Things went well for a bit, but T started getting possessive with me, but only where C was concerned. T wanted to know when I would be having sex with C; he was even asking about my sex with C, he wanted to know which one of them was the best. It got to a point where I didn't look forward to sex with him anymore, but then there was Thanksgiving, when I got there, T still had his uniform on and as soon as I walked in he slammed me against the wall and started frisking me, T had both my hands in one of his above my head. I was facing the wall, not knowing what's going on since T is so serious. He was touching me all over with one hand while his thigh was firm in between my legs. I thought the handcuffs were coming on, until he started groping my tits and saying that's how you liked them, big and firm, his hand slid down my stomach till he reached my pussy, he moaned because he could feel the wetness thru my shorts, yes people, I got wet while he was searching me. T turned me around in one sharp movement, now facing him, he kissed me and said this was a special arrest and we needed to do a full search, T starts to undress me while touching me all over, without letting go of my hands. That was so hot. But when T let go of me, then it got wild, we were all tired and sweaty when it was at last over, so tired I fell asleep, something I'd never done with T. Why? You ask. Well at least for me, it gets personal once you're actually sleeping together, sex is just that sex, but letting someone into your personal space, you're giving that person all of your trust, you're most vulnerable in your sleep, maybe you talk in your sleep or you snore, sleeping with someone leaves you completely open to them, and in my book, that's intimate and very personal.

Back to T. when I woke and saw what I'd done, I was dressed in 2 seconds flat, almost out the door, but T woke up before that. Talking about how lonely he felt, since women only used him for sex and no one actually slept with him like I had just done. I make it clear that it had been a mistake and that he felt that way because that's what he asked for and agreed upon as did I. in a way I felt sorry for him, because I really knew how it felt to be used and left. I kissed him and said my goodbyes before C came home.

Almost 6 months later and we are still in the same boat, only thing is C and I are sleeping together and it became more than just sex, but not enough for both of us to commit, he left his Porto Rican girlfriend and at that moment in time asked me to decide between him and T. That was one insane conversation, I just kept asking why? We are all happy in this arrangement; everybody is getting what they need. But his answer was enough to shut me up. C said, he was tired of listening to T brag about sex with me, he couldn't stand knowing that when he wasn't there T was sexing me, kissing me, touching my body and he just wanted it to stop, so he gave me that night to decide who I would stop seeing. Such a tough decision, I asked for a week, he said OK, but there was to be no sex from either of them until a decision was made and for real, that was not funny. Man. I have a soft, sensual, romantic man, who even bathes me and washes my hair, sexy as sin, we have sex all over the house and learns anything sexual I teach him and is also my best friend as well as my lover. On the other hand, I have this sexy, sexual beast, who gives me sex any which way I want, who is ready for me at the drop of a hat, this man is any woman's fantasy come to life. Just a little anecdote from each so you know why my decision is so damn tough:

With C, we had talked about videotaping, so one night I brought my camera and at first he kind of thought about it but then, he thought he was the director, I think that was the best, shortest sex we ever had, you started screaming CUT!, to no one and gave the chair where the camera was a spin. It was great fun and so sexy.

With T, we had just finished and were just lying in bed enjoying the aftermath of great sex, when the phone rings, he picks up, it's one of his booty calls, he tells her he needs 30 minutes, all the while he's on the phone he's touching my body and telling this girl how he was just dreaming about a woman with a butterfly tattoo on her chest (which I have) and how he was kissing it and sucking on her big titties (which I also have 42DD) and telling her how wet she was for him, and at that moment his hand slides down to my very wet pussy, now he tells her he has to go and that she has to wait 2 hours before coming over, then he hangs up so he can come finish what he started.

Now you tell me how I'm supposed to choose? Well that night I call T and tell him I have to choose and he had the same question I had, why? Starts asking me a thousand questions, who's better? Who will it be? Can we have some sex tonight? I told T I would let him know.

Early the next morning I called the man I wanted to stay with, because he needed to know first. I was totally unattached from the other, I would definitely miss the sex, but that was all, nothing more nothing less. I decided on the man whom I could have a conversation with as well as great, mind blowing sex, the one I could go out with, because we were friends as well as lovers. The one who I felt deep down in my heart, I was slowly falling in love with. Crazy huh? But most of the time it happens when you least expect it. My choice was Christian and from that day forward the only person from that house I had sex with was Chris (See how I specified from that house). T was mad for a while, but I think he knew it was more than just sex for C and me. We became friends afterwards. And I will always thank him for bringing C into my life for whatever time it lasted. You know what, I'll tell you all about my whole affair with Chris later, because right now I think I overdid my stay. And always remember, you get what you ask for, if it's only sex you want, let it be known, but please, if you want more, don't hide your feelings or play it off. Who knows what might come of it.........

Chastity 7

Lonely

It's so cold and dark, been raining all day. That's how I've been feeling lately, cold, dark and like crying. I've been so lonely, don't get me wrong, I have my family and friends, and of course, plenty of male companionship. But at this point in my life I want more, much more. I want a man to be there for me, which I feel has my back at all times, not only when it's convenient for him. I need him to be my anchor, so I don't keep drifting out to the open sea. I miss sleeping with a man, not just sexing him, I really mean sleeping, just cuddling in bed, making love whenever we want, and not when we can.

I've always been a sensual being, sexually I started later in life, but I have caught up. I'm a little sex devil and I need someone compatible with me or our needs will never be met. I'd say my biggest problem is that sexually, I give in too easy and too fast. See, my point of view is that if we enjoy each other's company, find one another attractive and sexually click, why wait? A lot of people don't agree with that, but to each his or her own opinion. My sexuality is mine and mine alone, do I share it? Yes, but only share, not one person can own who I am.

Have you ever been in a relationship where you forget who you are and just become someone totally different? I dare say it happens to most of us. You fall hopelessly in love with this great person and once you've been together for a few months, maybe even after many years, you see another side of that person and instead of accepting and coming up with a happy medium, you go and try to change them. Boy what a mistake!!! In time, the person changes, but then this isn't that person you fell in love with anymore and worst, they resent you for what you've made them do. And the love is gone, sadly sometimes all that love becomes the greatest hate of all.

Sometimes, we women, have a problem separating love and sex, men don't. We see sex as emotional glue, they see it as what it really is, SEX. As do I. maybe that's why I am alone. I've been told I'm a very intimidating woman and my sexual inhibitions, well probably don't help. But I'm tired of waiting for men to get the guts or be drunk enough to come up to me, so why not be me, the one to make the first move? Ask him to dance or send him a drink, just to start it all out. I'm woman enough to deal with the consequences. But to all the men out there reading my stories, listen very carefully, stop telling us you're going to call, when at that exact moment you're telling us you know you won't. Unless you are sexing a 16 year old, the rest of us, adult, mature women out there can handle the truth, maybe we are happy about not getting a call back, be truthful to us and yourself, we are adults. And girls, stop making these knucklehead men believe they're the bomb in bed, when they're not even a firecracker. Usually those are the ones calling and we are not picking up. This world is so mismatched. The men that rock your world, are usually players or married and we women that know what we're doing are looking for compatible men. What the fuck!! You know men go thru this also, they just don't talk about it, not even to their "boys", they'd rather say they're single because that's how they want it, we just straight out say, we're lonely. And they have the nerve to say we are the weaker sex, what a crock! Women go thru so much and yet we survive. Harder, tougher, untrustworthy towards men, but we are here. I've always said, "A woman, emotionally, becomes what a stupid, ignorant, unfaithful man makes her.

This is a bit of what made me hard.....................

I was 18 and thought I had met the most handsome, sexy, mature, Italian, older man, he was already 30, but also married, terrible marriage, a lot of problems he said. I was naïve but not stupid, so I asked his wife, she said it was all true, they were getting divorced. So I became the girlfriend of a married man, he was so sweet and romantic. But when we got to the sexual part of it, he was different, cold and hard. He made me give him oral sex all the time, pushing my head on to him, he even had anal sex with me, with no type of lubrication or notice, just pushed it in. Not even 2 months into the "relationship" I was pregnant, he was so happy, even though he already had 2 children and his "still" wife was also pregnant. It was all nice and dandy while I was pregnant, but as soon as I had the baby, he acted like it was just us, no baby. If you are a mother, you know how much that hurts, not just by any man but your child's father. I held on for 8 more months. When he told me to get packed so we could be together in The States for Christmas vacation, I told him the baby would need some winter clothes, he said he didn't mean for the baby to go, just me, he wanted me to leave him with my mom. And that was the last straw in the relationship, I left him. And people say, the older the more mature they are. Bullshit!

My second brush with pain, came a couple years later, it was a 13 year battle. I fell in lust with a tall, handsome Porto Rican. At first it was all sexual, even though he wasn't the best, he took care of business. I should have known it wasn't going to work from the get go, he was an alcoholic and women were drawn to him. But 4 months into the relationship I became pregnant, I was happy, I really had feelings for him at this point. Big mistake. First thing he told me was to get an abortion, I don't think so! I asked him to leave. He left for a few hours and came back asking me to forgive him, I did. We lived together and mostly happy the first 4 years. We had ups and downs, like every couple has, he cheated, I cheated back, but we remained together, mostly for the kids (at least that was my excuse), I really loved him. By this time he started seeing an ex-girlfriend he had from high school, even back then, she was the other woman, some things never change. Once he got her pregnant, he told me it was over between us. I told him he had to leave my home, he wouldn't, we lived under the same roof, slept in the same bed for a few more months and you guessed it, kept having sex. But every time sex was over with, he would just turn around and say, "This changes nothing". What a kick in the heart! But the women out there, who have gone thru this, know why we do it. We are just trying to keep him at home. Once he finally left the house, I couldn't stop crying; he'd come back for sex and just leave. I could never have a serious relationship with no one else, I kept saying that it was because of him, but it was really me, I didn't want to let go. Now I can tell you. After 13 years with this man, I thought I couldn't do better, that I wasn't worthy of a good man, I thought he was the best I could get. I was being disrespected, played and used by this man that kept saying he loved me, while he lived with another woman.

All this was done and over with as soon as I got back from overseas. By this time he was back living at his mother's home, but as soon as I got home, he came looking for me, he wasn't "able" to come see the kids, but a piece of chocha brings him in. Well he was greeted by the biggest bitch in the US Army. What a little sand does to a girl (and lots of time to think). As soon as he walked in the door, I asked him if he had come to fuck, he was stunned, since I never spoke to him like that before. We fucked, I came, it was over, he didn't finish, not my problem. No dick sucking, no kisses, no sweetness, everything straight and to the point. The love was gone, but me being a horny lil' bitch, I had to get mine and who better to do it with, than the man I had spent the last 13 years of my life with, he knew exactly how I liked it. But even sex wasn't enough to keep me there. Not even a year after I got back home, I told him to hit the road; I could do a lot better by myself. It was over for real and forever. At that moment it was the worst day of my life, now, I have to say it was the best decision I have made in my life. I don't want my boys growing up thinking that was the way to treat women. If I didn't learn to respect myself, how would my children respect me as a mother and a woman?

Well hopefully, now you see where I'm coming from, don't get me wrong, in no way or form do I hate men, oh no! I love them to death. I have 2 men in the making at home, I just pray that they never make a woman suffer for no reason, no woman deserves so much pain in 1 lifetime. Maybe that's why I'm still single, I'm not afraid of falling in love again, I'm afraid of falling out of it and somebody ending up hurt. Up to now, no man has made me feel secure enough to open up and give myself completely, the one that makes my heart flutter with just a look and sends shivers up my spine with a casual touch. The one I can trust my heart with and readily entrust my soul to. I believe in fate and that God has put a special person on this earth for each of us. Do you think it's possible that for some reason or another, we've turned that person away? I don't want to believe that, I know he's out there somewhere, just waiting for me. Going thru the trials of life, trying to make ends meet, maybe even trying in other relationships with children already as I have, but that wouldn't be a problem. So would you please come and find me, let's meet, get to know each other, fall in love and live happy together, (not that it will be that easy, but we can make it work). Come and embrace all I have to offer you as a good, trustworthy, sexy woman. I'm waiting for you.

Chastity 8

What's Cooking?

Well, well, well. Look whose back in the picture. My gorgeous, conceited chef. I've been waiting for you, waiting for a long time. I've thought about you a lot, about how silky your skin will feel under my touch, about how soft your lips will be when they kiss mine and mostly about how sweet that first kiss will taste. You really don't know how many times and ways I've imagined our first time go down. At the airport, in the car, everywhere possible in your house. I just don't know what it is about you, the sexy voice, beautiful smile, tight body or that arrogant, stuck up way in which you portray yourself. But see, I know better, I know that sweet, loving side, which not many people see. The real you, the one that comes out when we talk about your son, your family, employees, or just people you appreciate and love, I do think I know you pretty well. Do you realize how sexy it is to me, to listen to you being such a good father? How you like to spoil him and mostly, how much you love him. But let's get back to you, The Man.

I wish I knew why you feel the need to disappear from my life months at a time, but you want to know the funny thing about it? That I always accept you back in. You hear about it the first time we talk and that's it, everything is just like the last time we spoke. We have this strange thing going on, a connection of some sort. I feel like I can tell you almost anything (never everything), like we've known each other forever. I miss you so much at times, like when something exciting (as long as it has nothing to do with other men) or maybe a tragedy happens and I need to vent out, usually you are the first person I think of, you hear me out and even though you are far I feel better. Sometimes I will not call just because I don't want to bother you. Just like I know you vent out with me, about work, your family and friends, good things and bad. I believe that's why I feel so close to you. But if you only knew how much closer I want to get (In a way I've always thought you knew). I want to feel your heartbeat against my palm, your breath on my cheek, your hands on my body, how can I make you understand, I want you as a whole, the entire being that is you. You feel a lot of people (meaning mostly women) are just interested in what you got, but you have a woman right here, that is interested in all of you and really wants to help you make all your hopes and dreams come true. Do you know what the worst thing about all of this is? That, sincerely, from the bottom of my heart, I really don't think we will ever get to meet in person. And I really can't blame anyone, you have the money, but never the time (at least not for me), I would definitely make the time, but can't make it money wise. And I really do believe we are very good for each other, in every way. That's fate for you. I guess I'll have to settle with the phone calls; at least I get that much. This thing we have, 2 years this coming November, is something so special, at least to me, and truly that's the only reason I settle. There is one thing I want from you and that is to make my fantasy come true. How about it? You know where my mind goes when I think of you, straight to the gutter, I get down and dirty (filthy little mind of mine). Let's see what I can conjure up, not a difficult thing, since I've been playing it in my mind for a while now. Where will it be? I want it to be somewhere you haven't done it with anyone else before, I want this to be so special, even if it's just a onetime thing (really hope that's not the case). See, because ever since I met you, my sexy chef, I've been hungry for more than just your delicious food.

Let it all begin............

I go over for a long weekend visit. I arrive Thursday evening; we stay up most of the night talking, our first person to person, in real life conversation. Do you even realize how much I want to kiss you right now, feel you up close and personal? We both are kind of shy around each other, but we had a very nice conversation. But having you for real at last was enough for today, tomorrow will be something entirely different. I asked you to take me to your place of business before it opens and employees begin to arrive, I want to be there with you, all by ourselves. I want a full tour of the place and the last stop will be your kitchen. When we get to the grand kitchen, I can see how proud you are of what you have achieved, your chest swells as you show me around. I can't wait any longer, so I pull you towards me, reach for your neck and pull you down for a nice, long, soft kiss, but it doesn't stay soft for long.

You pull my body close to yours and now I can feel almost every part of your lean, strong body against mine. Your hands are now caressing my back, but go a bit lower to pull me even closer as if that was even possible. I can feel your hardness pushing against my belly. God, I want you so much right now!! You move me close to a table and sit me on it, now we are a bit more comfortable, since you are a bit taller than I all that making out has been a strain to my neck and your back, but I wasn't about to complain. But now the table helps me feel everything where I should've been feeling it. I wish I could've gone on kissing you, but I have to hurry before the employees start showing up. I grab your behind to pull you closer, now you are where I've wanted you all along. I grab your hand and guide it to my hot, wet kitty, she is so wet just by the kissing, now that you are touching her, oh my. We really need to get rid of some of these clothes or start unbuttoning, unhooking and unzipping some shit. This was already part of the plan, so I am dressed for it, very short skirt and a sexy top with no bra, so you got it easy. Now I just need to get you out of them pants and buried deep inside of me. I embrace your hips with my legs while my arms go around your neck. I want more. I want it all. I grab you, you feel so big, hard and thick, and you're taking too damn long. I bring down your zipper and take you in my hand, ohhhhh I've waited for this for so long. Your skin is so soft and yet your cock is rock hard. I want to taste you so badly, but no time now, got to save something for later. I pull you to me and slide my panty to the side, at last I can feel you, filling me completely, like this was how it was always meant to be. I guess you got bored of it on top of the table, so you grabbed me by the hips lifting me off of the table and slammed me against the wall, after about 20 minutes of intense fucking, I asked to be let down. I kissed you hungrily, it's like I can't get enough of you. I turn around and bend over your stove, put my skirt up and offer you what is already yours. You take me real hard for what seems like hours, but it's really only been a few minutes and then you cum fast and hard deep inside of me, it felt like coming home. I really don't know how many times I've cum, but for now it's enough. You show me to the back office, where we get cleaned up and out the door. Your people have already started coming in to work; you introduce me to a few. Most of them are smiling, like the cat that ate the canary, seems like everybody knew what we were doing a little while ago, not that I care either way. You kiss me on the cheek and just smile (Nice reaction). We have some lunch and head to your place. Where I get down to what I've been wanting to do since I laid eyes on you, taste all of you, time and time again.

Let's lay you in bed completely naked. You are so damn beautiful, love your tattoos, perfect body, at least in my eyes you are the most gorgeous man. Let me start off by kissing you, a lot of kissing, all the while I'm lying on top of you. I start by kissing your eyelids, cheeks, suck on your earlobe, bite your neck a bit, nibble on your nipples, I keep going further down, your stomach is so lean I have to lick it, but I want something else……… something that will repress my hunger, for a bit at least………… There it is……… ………… I kiss you there………… Lick a little…….…………. Suck a little………………… and then … ………………………….. Hopefully you will find out sooner rather than later (Really do hope you do). Because pa, you need to give me something to work with…………..

Chastity 9

In Da Club

I know a lot of ya'll have done this, so don't be frontin' on me. I'm totally sure you've had a little bathroom action or some handling under the table or at an out of the way booth at a bar or club, or maybe even better, a dark corner out in the open. So let's see what I thought out or maybe I have done this, who knows.

Babe, how about a sexy date? We can just make believe, role play, however you want to call it. If you've read my other stories, you know I kind of get off on the stranger thing, so for this we will make believe we don't know each other. We are going to pick out a town out of the way, where no one knows us and let the fun begin.

We pick a town about an hour away, we take separate cars, because you will be leaving about an hour before I do, I want you to get the feel of the place, have a few drinks, check out the girls and just act like your there by yourself, which you will be. But the biggest reason, I want to see your face when you see me walk thru that door, looking all hot and sexy. My hair is naturally curly, so I go with that, make up to a minimum, nice natural look, only eyes and lips have a bit. Nice white top, one that accentuates my breasts, no bra, so you can literally see my nipples and since I'm so excited about all this, I know they will be at attention all night. A very short, black skirt, nice black, lace g-string, if I bend over everybody would be able to see my ass. And last but not least, black, thigh high, stiletto boots, my legs look so long and lean. Tonight I want everyone to look at me; I'm going to be the center of attraction. We agreed there would be no communication after you left the house, so you wouldn't know exactly when I'd be arriving or what I'd be wearing, which was a plus. I took a bit more time than planned, just so you wouldn't be expecting me. My car was nice and clean, my sound system was booming, everyone is looking my way once I get there, but since my windows are tinted they can't see who it is. I find a great parking space right in front. Expectation was high, so why make them wait any longer. Men and women alike were waiting for me to get out of my car, as soon as my black boot was on the floor, women were like "whatever", but men couldn't stop staring, they made may for me to walk in, as soon as I was inside, all eyes were on me. Even the bartender offered me a drink with his phone number on the napkin. I took it. Great way to start out my night, with a good, strong tequila sunrise.

Looks like you're having a good time also, you're in the back playing some pool, got a sexy little thing all over you. Still haven't seen me, but you will soon enough. I go up to the disc jockey and ask him to play something really sexy for me to dance to. I reach out to a very nice looking, big, black man, I've been watching, so I know he can dance. We take the floor and just get down and dirty, (I should get into the stripper business), he doesn't back down, he's with me all the way. People stop dancing to stare at us, what a little show we are putting on. Now I'm sure I have your attention, so I start kissing my dance partner, a real sexy ass kiss, his hands start roaming my body. One girl yelled we should get a room, but don't think so, I have other plans. The song is over and I say thank you and bid him farewell, he looks at me like I'm crazy, but I just say "it was just a dance." I walk up to the bar, where my favorite bartender serves me another drink and compliments my dancing, I say thank you and blow him a kiss. You are standing at the bar, up, close and personal with your new lady friend, the girl really wants you bad. The bar area is pretty dark, so I bend down a moment and when I come up, it's on. I wink at the bartender, then step in between of you and your little friend, French kiss you, when I'm quite satisfied with the kiss I back away, but before going anywhere, I stuff my panties in your mouth and then walk back to the dance floor. When I look back, the girl is kind of pist off, but you and my bartender friend are just smiling. I grab a guy and start dancing, you cut in, grabbing me from behind, your arms go around my waist, and you nibble on my neck and a whole lot of grinding goes on. We don't talk, just going with the flow of the music. Your hands move up to my breasts, pinching my nipples with your fingers, you are doing this even though you know what it does to me. Turn me around to face you, bring your hand down between our bodies while we kiss, it slides down to my pussy, which is already so wet, your other hand goes into my hair, which is pulled back while your mouth goes to my neck again. Goodness! That hand is taking me to the edge. I bite down on my lip, grab your hand, suck on your finger that tastes of me and lead you back to the bar where we have another drink. I'm calm now, still horny and so wet; but calm. We start kissing again, but you stop it, just long enough to get to a dark, lonely booth in the back of the club Move the table a bit, just to make it more comfortable, then you sit me on your lap, you're so damn hard, now you start whispering in my ear that it's all my fault, for dancing, kissing other men, flirting with the bartender, but mostly for the little scene in front of the other girl which ended with very wet panties in his mouth. I pout my lips like a little girl and in a sexy whisper tell you how sorry I am, start sucking on your earlobe, while I ask again, if there is something I can do to make it up to you. You grab my pussy, while you say you want sex right here, right now. You know me; always want to keep my man well satisfied, anywhere, however and whenever. I stand up, unzip you, and bring your beautiful, big cock out. Sometimes I think I'm with you just because of how big and thick you are, also sex is always great. I sit on your lap again, this time taking you all in, you always feel so good; at the same time your hand is doing wonders on my clit. I'm about to explode, but not without you, never without you. I grab your testicles and pull softly, while with my other hand I pull you closer by the nape, to kiss you while we cum together. And what better to push us to the edge, than knowing that your new friend and my cute, sexy bartender are watching us from the bar. That just did it for me, it was like an explosion, I felt it all over my body, my screams were disguised by the music and were engulfed in your kiss. I love the way you take me all in. You grabbed my hips pulling me down on you, feeling you deeper inside, I felt your cum pumping in me, so warm. Then we just sat there a few minutes, basking in the aftermath of incredibly great sex. Walk into the men's bathroom together, guys stare, but I guess, they don't really mind. We get cleaned up and sit at the booth again for a bit. Been a while since you've fucked me like this, so raw. But babe, we're not done yet. I want more, when it comes to you, I'm never completely satisfied.

I bid you farewell with a peck on the lips and strut away. You just stare after me, watching other men turn around just so they can look at my firm derriere. I know you like it when other men look at me with their eyes full of lust, mostly because you know that at the end of the night, you'll be the one holding me in your arms, with your dick deep inside of me. I go to the bar, pull my bartender by the shirt and give him one hell of a kiss before walking out of the club. When you come out, you notice my car still parked out front, you scan the lot and see me sitting on the hood of your car, smiling you walk towards me, open the door of the car and sit back. I laugh, but go to you. I straddle you while we kiss for a bit, get off and sit on the passenger's seat, open your pants, take your dick out again, but this time, I gently kiss the head, then I take it whole. I know how you like it pa, suck it hard and gently nibble. You cum for me, so warm in my mouth, you always taste so sweet. Lick my lips; get out of your car and straight into mine. We drive off together, talking on the cell phone until we arrive to our destination, which is................home. Start taking our clothes off from the front door and jump in the shower together, we bathe each other (another thing I enjoy of this relationship we have), you wash my hair (that there is sexy), when we are done, I wrap a towel around my breasts, you wild thing just step out nude (God I love your body). Air conditioner is blasting, we jump in bed and we are once again a happy couple, you are my baby. Right now, all I want from you is to be able to fall asleep in your arms while we cuddle. And you never disappoint me, as I am falling asleep with my head on your shoulder and your arms around me, I bid you good night, remind you how much I love you and let your alter ego know, "Till our next sexy adventure."

Chastity 10

Unforgettable Night

Oh my Goodness what a night!!! And who would have thought I'd be spending it with these people. But let's start from the beginning.

It was a Friday night when I received the call from my dear friend Lyn, you guys remember her, huh? Well anyways, she's spending some time with a very good friend of hers and a friend of his (at his house), this other friend, well I met him a few years back on one of my many trips with the military and really liked him from the get go, but nothing came of it and now he's here, on my turf. But Friday I couldn't do anything about it, first, I was so tired, had been at work at 6am, then to school at 5pm, I was just getting home when she called me at about 11pm, and secondly, I had one of my sons with me and wasn't going to leave him by himself. But then she told me she'd probably be staying there all weekend. I already had plans for Saturday, but things change. I went to work, met the guy I had a date with, told him I had a get together which was already planned and had to go (it was the truth), but left him wanting to see me again. Went to my high school class reunion, but stayed only a couple of hours. Went home took a shower, shaved everything (now it's all nice and smooth), washed my hair, got all oiled up, put on a little short skirt, nice brown blouse (no bra), very comfy sandals, packed an overnight bag and out the door I went. Kids were in their respective grandmother's house, so the night was mine.

My girl was giving me directions on the phone, until my new victim took the phone and got me there himself. He was waiting for me at the entrance of his place. I got out of my car and straight into his arms, he gave me a nice peck on the lips, everything felt damn good and so natural between us, like we had been a couple for a while and yet we hadn't even talked about anything romantic or sexual before. We walked up to his place hand in hand. There I met up with my girl and her man, hellos were said, drinks were made and drank, and beers were thrown into the pool. Everything was so cool and relaxing. It was like, it was only us 4, nobody else, the house and pool were in complete darkness. We were standing by the veranda kissing and touching, when he reached down and started taking off my panties and the craziest thing is that I just let him, even though our friends were just a few feet away. He asked me to go to the pool with him, he had shorts on, my girl told me she had an extra bathing suit I could use, I let them know mines was in my car, but he just said, "no worries, you won't be needing it, you're going as you are." Hmmm, that sounds like trouble. But yet again, I did as he asked, a bit weird for me, since I'm used to being in control of the situations I get myself into. But there was a whole lot of drinking going on, so I'll blame the rum on this one. Once we got to the pool, he took off his shorts and started pulling and pushing mine off, I was a bit against it, since I do have this reticence (hang up) about my belly. It's not the same thing being in a dark room doing what you know you can do very well, than being out in the open with other people around, even though my girl has seen my naked before, but her man hasn't. I think at this exact moment roles were reversed and I became the victim, because it was like he had some special power over me or something, because off came the clothes and into the pool we went.

This man is literally, the type of man every woman dreams of, handsome, tall, single, spontaneous, a true gentleman (opens the doors for you), very tender, doting, great sense of humor, so affectionate and did I say he's single and has a good paying job? Is this man even possible? Can he be for real? If I didn't know better, I or any other woman out there could fall in love with this man. But as I do know better, he is probably a low down dog like most of them players out there, so I can't let myself fall for his charm and charisma.

Anyway, back to the good stuff. We are in a dark pool, all by ourselves, naked. Like I said before, he is tall and has a very lean, beautiful body (not skinny). He asked me to hug him and wrap my legs around his waist, now we were really feeling each other. My foreigner isn't a big man in the dick department, but he compensates in so many other ways. Even though we were naked, we didn't have sex at that time; we played with each other and kissed A LOT. The man is so damn thoughtful (that is sexy), always asking if I needed or wanted something to drink and always asking me if I was comfortable with him. That was funny, since I was fucking naked, in the dark, with only him (which I really didn't know well), did he really think that if I wasn't comfortable I'd still be there? Don't think so. Lyn and her friend went out to get more ice and things kind of heated up with us. He sat me on the edge of the pool, spread my legs and just ate me there in the dark, with the only light being the brightness of the stars. It was absolutely mind blowing. Can you believe this was a first for me? (SHUT UP!!!) It was. Got back in the water and kissed some more, ohhh can he kiss. He still didn't want to give me any sex, but the man sure liked the pussy, because once again I was on my back and he was getting his fill. The other couple came back and he went upstairs to get me a towel and a robe. We had a beer with them and chilled, all this and many kisses in between. Every time either of us got up for anything the other would go also. It was sweet and sexy. In one of our turns to get the drinks, I stepped away from him towards the dining room, so I could go check my cell, when he turned me around, opened the robe and kneeled before me, which was really breath taking. He put my foot on top of a chair and had his hands on my hips supporting me. It was crazy since we knew anyone could come in at any moment, he wanted more, so he stood and pulled me to a closed off balcony, took off my robe, laid it on a sofa there, then laid me on top. Still not giving me the sex that I already needed so badly, but he was satisfying me orally. He kept saying I tasted so good he couldn't help himself. And I wasn't about to start complaining about that. We went outside a bit later, finally with the drinks, talked a bit, kind of took a break from each other, I spoke to Lyn while he talked to his friend. Then he wanted to go back to the pool again. He was acting so damn sweet, wouldn't let me go for nothing. Not even to go get a beer, I'd have to go with him, but that always was a good thing, we would always kiss, touch and so much more. Mmmmm I was going to my car to get my bathing suit, since the 4 of us were going into the pool now, but he wouldn't let me, he wanted me in one of his shirts and that's what I wore. (I'm sounding like a wuss with this guy). We all got in the pool, but each couple to his own side of the pool, the lights were on, but that didn't last long, my man was getting aggravated with me still having so much clothes on, so there went the lights and with the lights my shirt, my man was back in the water and all over me. He laid me back in the water, putting a hand on my chest and just swaying my body from side to side, watching my hair flow in the water. All the stars were shinning bright in the sky. I felt sexy and loved. (This is definitely not good). The first time I felt this great looking guy deep inside me, was at about 3am, while my girl was having her own fun, this went on till about 5:30am. I was freezing already, but didn't want to sound soft in front of my man, but enough is enough, I told him and he just told me to hug myself to him, (which I've been doing all night), but babe I'm still cold, he went upstairs (naked), to get my robe and then we went up to the house, jumped in bed and there we go.

I love the way this man kisses me, he touches me just right. He doesn't see my body the way I do, for him it's beautiful. He bites, licks and sucks me all over. God!!!!!! He does things to me that just drive me crazy. More oral sex and he deep inside are about all I need at the moment. We had been up since early the day before, so when he fell asleep during sex, I was a bit disappointed, but he caught himself quickly, apologized profusely and got the job done and very well if I say so myself. We fell asleep together and cuddling. We didn't even sleep for 5 hours, I woke up first, cuddled next to him and started kissing and nibbling him, but he was knocked out. I went to the bathroom and not even 5 minutes later he was out of the room looking for me (so cute). I went back to the room, laid on top of him and there we go again, we sexed during the day with lots of light and he still wanted more (my inhibitions are almost out the window with this man). Went to my car, got my stuff, so I could take a shower and go out and get some grub. So hungry. Took a shower together (surprise), lots of kissing and back to bed for more sex, took another shower with very cold water. Told him to stay as far away from me as possible, can't have him near me without kissing or touching him, but as I was getting dressed, he saw my panties (sexy little thing really) and he took them off and once again there we go. Me with some of my clothes on, him naked, sexing like bunnies. I could go at it all day and night with this guy (which was kind of what was already happening). Stop!!! Took a quick shower by myself and at last we left, my girl and her main squeeze had already left. We were going in his vehicle; he opened the door for me and helped me in. While driving he held my hand, (felt like I had a boyfriend). We found our friends on the way and since they had bought food for all of us we turned back. My girl said I couldn't live of sex alone, but I could definitely try. We had lunch together; he served me my food and drink, made sure I was ok. When I went inside to get my phone, we were picking up some things left on the table and probably by mistake he picked up some woman's clothing, which wasn't mine or my friends, just then, he knew he was in trouble. Right at that moment everything changed (good for me, since I was falling fast and hard). I made believe I didn't care and just lead him to the bedroom, where we had some more great sex and then just fell asleep once again. I enjoy being with him so much its crazy. We woke up almost at the same time, took a nice cold shower together and I threw myself on the bed with just the towel on, he came over and spread my legs and more sex, this one was a quickie, my baby couldn't take me moving for him, he asked me to give him a second so he could get in a fast shower and a few minutes later, there he was again, in all his naked glory (such a beautiful body). I was lying across the bed, my head to the side where he was standing, he asked me to give him my pussy, but this time I wasn't doing as I was told. I grabbed him by his hips and brought him to my mouth, thought he was going to fall back. Took him all in my mouth, he tastes so good, he didn't let me finish him off with my mouth, instead he turned me around and did me real good, but again he came almost immediately. He calls me his Kryptonite. We couldn't do anything else, because our friends wanted a bit of our attention and really, we had fucked all night and most of the day away already. So we went out to the pool and interacted with our friends (we were behaving like boyfriend and girlfriend), until I couldn't stand it anymore and while our friends were busy in the pool, I took his dick out of his pants and sucked him nice and good, right there. Just a moment later they decide to get out of the damn water, we were looking crazy and just started laughing. It's about time to go home, he doesn't want me to leave and I don't want to go anywhere, but that's life. Start picking up my stuff, all the while, hugging and kissing. Walks me to my car, we kiss and talk about a next time. Do you think there'll be a next time? I really don't know. Why not? Well maybe because I really like the guy and let's not even mention our banging sexual chemistry (out of this world). But what if I want more and he doesn't? It would really hurt, so why risk it. Let's just keep it on the low, getting together once or twice every few months and just doing what we do best, have lots and lots of great sex, while I fantasize about being the only woman in your life at the moment (for at least a day or so). We'll see what happens next time, maybe some other 1st for me.

Chastity11

Far, Far Away

Here we go once again, but this time I will explain this thing I have about strangers. See, the thing is, that if you get with a stranger, you don't have to worry about their emotional, financial or personal life or them yours, it's just plain fun and sex. And if you know or just think that you will never encounter this person again (baby the gloves come off), sex is so much better. Because there's no inhibitions what so ever, you're not even thinking about what your body looks like naked (pot belly, ugly feet or small tits). And all the things you've wanted or dreamed about doing but haven't because you haven't dared, you can and will with this person. That's my obsession with strangers. But this time there's a bit of a twist. I'm on vacation!

Vacation time is here at last, school is out, and kids are with their fathers. Time for myself. I have some money put away, so I plan my vacation carefully. Where have I always wanted to go? Someplace different, not in Latin America or United States. Hmmm Europe? All by myself in such a faraway place. I don't know. But what a rush it would be. I do need some adventure in my life. I go to the travel agency and book a 3 week stay; this includes airline tickets, hotel and meals there. So now I guess I'm on my way to France. The only thing I really don't like is the long plane ride ahead, but I will make sure it's well worth it. On the plane I meet many interesting people, some much more interesting than others, that always happens and more so when you have so many hours with not that much to do in between. I always have plenty of reading material and of course my pen and paper, in case something pops up in this sexy little mind of mine, can't go nowhere without my music, lots of that. I'm in a window seat, just chilling' since there was nobody seated in the seats beside me. Got comfortable, read a bit, heard music some and then just out of nowhere, this beautiful man asks if he may sit by me. French accent, pale complexion, sky blue eyes, blond hair, very tall and the most delicious looking lips I've seen in a long time. I caught myself staring at his mouth and tripped over a simple yes for his question. We introduced ourselves and explained each other's trip to this marvelous country, mine, well a very old dream finally coming true, since I've wanted to go forever. His, well going home after a very long hiatus in the United States for his education. After talking for what seemed like hours, I yawn, not because I'm bored, far from it, but I am very tired and when I look at my watch I see why, it's almost 11:00pm, been a very long day. Ask if he doesn't mind me sleeping for a bit, his answer was so sweet, "My shoulder is your pillow Madam." I ask the flight attendant for a blanket and pillow, so do you, we get comfortable and I fall asleep in Pierre's arms. Crazy! I don't know how long I slept, but it felt like a few hours. I felt myself getting aroused, my nipples hardening and my kitty is ready, as I slowly awake. I can feel Pierre softly caressing my arm and hand so innocently, but my body was responding in such a wicked manner. His eyes are still closed, the cabin is very dark since mostly everybody is asleep and their lights are out. So, I take his hand and put it on my breast and just wait out his response. Will he accept what I'm offering or go back to his seat? He comes close and whispers in my ear, "I cannot offer you anything more than this at the moment." My answer was so simple, "I'm not asking for more than that." Just then his beautiful, soft lips cover mine in an amazing, toe curling, and breathtaking kiss. I was taken aback with just a kiss. My first French experience and I'm not even in France yet. Our hands start roaming each other's body, a bit clumsy, since we really don't have a lot of space and then also trying to keep quiet, being that we are surrounded by people. But once his hand finds my oh so wet pussy, I forget where I'm at and a low moan escapes my lips, that second he captures it with his mouth and at that same moment he plunges 2 fingers deep inside me. I grab at him trying to bring him closer to me, which works; my head is against the window and my left leg on the seat. He has situated himself between my legs. He crawls under the blanket and takes a breast out and start sucking while he keeps fingering me vigorously. I already feel my orgasm a nip away, it came when he introduced a third finger and bit my nipple, Oh My!! He held on until my spasms stopped, smiling down at me like a Cheshire cat. I'm a bit shy after the facts, but only for a few moments. I ask him to excuse me a moment to go to the ladies room. At my return he is right where I wanted him to be, his back against the window, eyes closed, but his lips curved in a sexy smile as if remembering what just occurred. Before he can register what's happening, I have unbuttoned and unzipped him and his penis is in full attention just for me. Now it's my turn. I go under the blankets and taste him for the first time, damn he's delicious. I go at it while his hands caress my back, shoulders, when he's about to cum his hands snake up into my hair and grab on for dear life. He whisper, "Le petit mort", I've heard this before, translated it means "little death", which in France is used for orgasm. He tastes so sweet. I stay on his chest for a few minutes, but then let him get up to go get himself cleaned up. He brings me back some moist wipes and a bottle of water, I clean myself there and both satisfied at this moment and fall asleep in each other's arms once again. Slept for about 3 hours, woke up to share breakfast, while we talked about everything under the sun for the last 2 hours of our flight. We exchanged numbers so we could finish what we started. A kiss good-bye on the plane.

And now I am really ready to start my adventure in France.

I went to my hotel to rest for a while, everything in its place and slept a few hours, took a shower, put on some comfortable street clothes (nothing to shabby) and out to explore. This 1st afternoon I'm staying near the hotel, want to find my way around before having to catch a cab or call the hotel because I got lost. At about 9:30pm I find myself in front of this cute little quaint bistro a few streets away from the hotel. I decide it's a great place to have dinner at and people watch. I had a delicious Steak Au Poivre with a sweet glass of Cremant DuJura (French wine). I'm trying to have a taste of France here, since I didn't come all the way here to eat hamburgers or pizza. I sit in a small table outside with a Café Bonbon and a croissant, just watching people walk by and writing down my thoughts. People here are just beautiful, their language is beautiful, their accent and even the way they treat you. This will be a great vacation. My waiter brings me a cordial called the Black Rose and a beautiful rose painted black, he said, "Nothing should upstage your beauty on such a splendid evening in which I have finally found you belle." He knows how to make a girl blush and to boot, he is totally handsome. But still I told him I hadn't ordered anything; he said it was from him to me and to enjoy the "douceur de vivre." The drink was delicious. I sat there for about a 1 ½ hour, when he came out took my hand, pulled me to my feet, embraced and kissed me passionately.

At first I was perplexed but that quickly faded and I start kissing him right back, he just pulled back and said let's go. I just stared at him, he said he'd explain on the way, as we started walking he told me he told his boss I was his girlfriend that had come all the way from the USA to see him, so that his boss wouldn't say anything about the free drink and of course letting him leave earlier to be with me, I just laughed about it. When I asked the why of the kiss, he said "Well, first to make it more credible and second, I've been wanting to ever since you came thru the doors." What more explanation did I need? I told him I really didn't want to venture too far from the hotel and really, I don't know this guy, but it's in adventure and that's what I'm here for. It's not like I have anyone else to go out with. He took me to some nice places nearby, not letting me pay for anything, translating the drinks names and the contents in them, just so I would know (very considerate of him). Mostly everywhere we went American hip-hop or dance music was being played, guess that's how we got it. It was a blast; he is just so much fun. When I looked at my watch, to my surprise I see it's already 4am and I still don't even know his name, but something I do know, is that I want him. We start walking back to the hotel when he gives me some much needed information, he's 25 years old (or young however you want to see it), 6 feet tall, 190lbs, he's a Scorpio and most importantly, his name is Yan, then he asks, " Voulez vous coucher aver mo ice soir?" I'm looking at him like a teenager in lust, just his accent has me wet, even though I don't know what the fuck he said, I really don't care. I grab him by his collar, pull him in for a kiss and say "oui" to whatever he said. He laughs and opens the hotel door for me. We go up to my room, which from now on will be my lucky number "810". He takes the key card from my hand, opens the door and led me in; all the while his thumb is caressing my palm in a good way. I went to stand by the window looking out to this beautiful view of the City of Lights, made more wonderful by having him behind me, kissing my neck, stroking my arms, nibbling on my ear. I turn around in his arms, grab his face and my tongue does the talking, this way we understand each other fabulously. He pushes my body against the cold window and while we make love with our mouths, he loves me with his hands; they're all over me, as soon as his hand reaches my breasts, and he starts whispering in my ear in his native tongue, Oh My God!! I don't think I can handle this. My body is responding like never before to this erotic, foreign foreplay. About to cum and we haven't even touched intimately (other than my tits). His thigh gets comfortable in between my legs and that did it, my 1st orgasm with Yan, he just smiles, kisses me, pats my behind and pushes me toward the bed. He sits and starts giving instructions "Turn on radio but not too loud and start undressing for me very slowly. I want to see you completely naked." And I did as I was told. Felt a bit vulnerable as I was completely nude while he was fully clothed, but in a way also felt in control when I saw how his eyes were eating me all up and how his hard cock stood at attention just for me and because of me. Not a word, not a sound other than the soft music in the background and our heavy breathing. I kneel down in front of him, bring his zipper down, oh my look at this, he's commando (for those of you who don't know the term, it means no underwear), his dick immediately makes its way thru, precum glistening the head and I indulge my need to lick it all up, nice and tangy, not bad. I play with him for a while, but he stops me, muttering something in French, "merde", grabs me by my arms and pulls me up, takes off all his clothes in record time, pushing me face first into the bed and take me roughly from behind, grabbing my hair and pulling towards him so he could take my mouth at the same time he pounds into my throbbing, wet pussy. Our tongues communicating in one simple language, lust, pure and simple. I think I'm falling in love with these French men; they seem to just love, fucking, sucking, licking and everything in between. Lustful men for a sexy, lustful me, couldn't have gone to a better place for my vacation. We go at it for hours, he is just insatiable and the man knows exactly what he's doing, keeps me wet the whole time. Yan is the type of guy that makes you feel special, he made sure I felt taken care of; my needs were satisfied many times over before his. I came with his cock, fingers, mouth and many other objects available around my room. Its lunch time already and we are just getting out of the shower and of course had sex in there. While we were flat out exhausted in bed I order us some lunch and you keep kissing my back and nibbling my thighs. I cannot go one more round with him right now, so tired. We doze off until room service knocks on the door; you get it with just a towel wrapped around your waist. You are so damn sexy! I feel myself growing wet again, can't believe it. We feed each other; you grab your dessert, eating me until I cum as many times as you want me to.

Yan calls his boss and tells him he needs a few days off to show me around town and he gets them, but today I think we will sleep in and of course having lots of sex. The next few days were spent like tourists;

he took me to so many fabulous places I've always wanted to go to, like Avenue des Champs Elysees, Eiffel Tower (where we necked like teenagers), Louvre Museum, Arc de Triumphe, Moulin Rouge, Notre Dame, Chateau de Versaille which is one of the largest castles in France, there we found a dark little room and what started out as a simple touching session, became a full on sex session, we were both standing when you slipped my panties to the side and entered me from behind (beginning to think you really like it like that) and I just couldn't resist grinding into your hard cock and knowing we have to hurry, I move just like you like so we can hurry this along. You cum so hard in me I almost scream your name. But held on. We clean up and find the rest of the group again. Our last place was a trip down River Seine for an evening trip that was the most romantic thing ever, beautiful scenery, full moon shinning on the river, handsome company that doesn't leave me untouched for more than 2 minutes. I knew this was the last night I would spend with Yan, he's taken me to most the tourist sites I wanted to see, we've eaten in the best restaurants (on him, really doesn't let me pay for much) and my, the sex only gets better with this man. But I still have 2 weeks of vacation time and want some time on my own to look around. But I will definitely see him before I leave, that is a fact. We have a very late dinner (light), tonight is a bit bittersweet, since we know after this he will not be staying with me every night. We'll keep in touch, just not daily. (I'll make sure of that by changing rooms). He says "just lay back and let me pamper you." He gets some oil and starts with my feet, then my calves, behind my knees was erotic all by itself, then my thighs, softly his hands caressed and made love to my thighs, just when I thought he'd start on my honey pot, he stopped and went to my feet again, where he kissed and sucked every toe, then my heel, arch, ankle, all the way up to my thigh again, but you didn't go straight to my hot spot. You tease me and start licking the tattoo on my hip (that tickles), suck on my waist and stomach, then he stalls again and instead of sucking my sensitive, waiting breasts, he went for my shoulder and neck (this guy is a genius). He takes my mouth and kisses me like this is the last time, well at least that's what I let him think. This time he wants to make love to me and I let him, I've been wanting so badly for someone to pamper me like he has. Thank God I'm in charge and know not to let myself go. This is just a fantasy, a vacation, something to hold on to and remember when I'm lonely at home. Was a very beautiful and satisfying moment (like always with Yan). In the morning he greets me with a kiss and breakfast in bed. I see all his belongings by the door. I guess this is good-bye to my waiter (for now). He lays next to me while I drink my coffee, just looking at me as if he wants to burn my image in his memory. He then says, "Je ne regretted rien." Kisses me softly on the lips and gets up to leave, I let him. I wish he'd say all those things in English, just so I could understand, but maybe it's for the best. Blows me a kiss from the door and says "Je t' adore." I smile and he's gone. (Already miss him)

What a wonderful vacation it has been, just a few days before I need to head back to my island (Bummer). But can't complain everything was better than I could've dreamed or imagined. After Yan left I missed him, but not enough to bring him back just yet. I spent a couple of days on my own, just taking in the beauty of it all, this place really blows me away. People are so outspoken, men and women were asking me out, had dinner with one guy, out to a café with another, but no sex, just nice conversation and a bit of flirting, (maybe 1 or 2 kisses and some touching), but that's it. A few days into my self-imposed solitude, I receive a surprise call, who else but Pierre. He's done doing the family thing and wants to come to Paris to spend some time with me (long weekend), of course I said yes. Want to finish what we started on the airplane. God and did we finish, to just start everything all over again many times over. The weekend seemed so short I just couldn't believe it; we mostly stayed in the room. Other than the sex being so great we didn't want to leave the bed, I also didn't want Pierre to run into Yan, since I still had some plans with him. If I had to choose between my French lovers, I really wouldn't be able to, they each have their own way of driving me mad in lust, I can't choose. But back to the man at hand. Pierre went all out our last night together, had a hot, bubble bath drawn for me with white rose petals (which made me think of Yan's black ones) and scented oil. He bathed me, while kneeling outside of the Jacuzzi, giving me kisses in between of washing my hair and rinsing it, he left me alone so I could soak in the warm water for about 15 minutes, and then came to get me. As soon as I stood up, he had a white silk robe waiting. As we walked hand in hand towards the main suite, I can already smell the food and even the smell was delicious, my stomach started rumbling, we just started laughing. It was all finger food, which he fed me as I laid in bed, felt so good to be taken care of. After I had my share of food and nibbling on Pierre, he started giving me a foot massage, I was almost asleep, that is until he started sucking on my toes (now I'm really awake). We had the most passionate sex, not even what we did on the plane can compare; it was erotic, exotic and so sexy. His mouth tasted every part of my body, not one part went without being savored, it was as if he wanted to engrave in his mind every expression, moan and movement my body did while he had his way with me. Satisfied, sated and sweaty we fall asleep, with him still hard and deep inside my love. Woke up in the same position, he's already going at it, while kissing my neck and pinching my nipples, this is the best way to wake up. I felt like I came a thousand times in just a few minutes, he made me feel complete. But like everything, it has come to an end and it's time for Pierre to go home. After we took a quick shower and have a light breakfast, we exchange numbers, e-mail and physical addresses. It's a bittersweet moment, but we knew it would come to this. Long, soul baring kiss and bye bye Pierre. Lots of things to fantasize about when I get home, how did I get so lucky?

Well, how do I spend my last two nights in Paris? I surely know I want to go to a club tonight and dance until the morning. I'm definitely not going alone, so I'm on my way to go find my boo, Yan. I want to spend my last night's with him and fuck him till I'm about to get on that damn plane. I didn't call, I walked down to the café he works at and asked for him to be my waiter, I was told he wouldn't be in for another 30 minutes, so I asked for a salad while he got there. Guess his boss called him because he was there in 10 minutes flat, came to my table and kissed me right there, asked for my order (me being how I am), told him I just wanted him, but I would wait till he got off work. Asked for something lite and ate outside so I could watch the beautiful sunset unfold, while waiting for a beautiful, sexy man. We had some fun while he worked, like me grabbing his butt when he walked by me and him following me to the bathroom, where I gave him a quick but very enjoyable blowjob, didn't let him go until he gave me all that delicious cum. It was lots of fun, flirting with him like this. When he finally got off work, we walked to his apartment a few blocks away to get some clothes for the couple of nights he'd be staying with me. Once there, Yan wasted no time, closed the door and slammed me against it (sexy, I like it rough), touches me all over while kissing me roughly, his hand finally reaches my pussy which is already so wet, he moans while pulling my panty to the side and slamming his fingers in me, I'm about to cum right then and there but he kneels and puts my leg on his shoulder and really goes to work on my kitty. Mmmmm so sweet. Now, I'll cum for him, so he can taste my juices. He seems to be enjoying this almost more than I am (and I'm receiving), he is just too sexy for his own good. My legs begin to tremble, it's all too much to hold on, even though my back is against the door, I can't stay upright. As soon as I cum, the juices he doesn't lick up with his tongue begin running down my thighs, and even with his shoulder below my leg and his strong hands on my hips can't hold my body from sagging down the door. He is there to grab me in his arms and hold me till these great sensations and the trembling of my body subsides. Then he just carries me in to the shower and bathes me gently, while he kisses my body all over. As soon we are done in the shower, he tells me we need to go, so we can get ready and start partying. We start off at a nice, out of the way place with great music. We dance all night together and with other people, we flirt around but know with whom we arrived and whom we will be leaving with. I love how it feels to be out and about with Yan, he is beautiful, exotic, funny, intelligent, sensual, and sexual, everything I'd want in a man (too bad we live so far away). We never left the first place; we stayed until the sun came up and were told to leave. We got back to the hotel at about 9am, had breakfast in the hotel restaurant and straight up to my room. Once there we jump in to the Jacuzzi, I sit with my back against it and him between my legs, wrap my legs around his waist and just feel each other and the jets soothing our bodies, we just caress one another till we fall asleep, right then and there. We wake because the water has turned cold, just to jump in the bed, have a quickie and fall asleep in each other's arms. We awaken early evening and decide to stay in since it's the last night of my vacation and of our little love affair. Literally stay in bed all evening, watching movies, making love, just touching each other, talking, kissing all night. It would be so easy to fall in love with this man, but I can't and I will not. But this is something that I will treasure for the rest of my life, he will always be my lover from Paris, the man I loved and left behind. We wake up early and make love for the last time and just lay in bed not even speaking just taking each other in. I just want to touch him and take home the feel of him, the warmth of his skin. I want to taste him and always remember his tangy taste on my tongue. I just want to look at him and remember every detail about his body, like his gorgeous eyes and smile, his firm hands, strong legs and of course his beautiful, big cock. I will never forget my Yan.

Well, it's that time. Yan goes with me to the airport and we say our sad good byes and kiss at the gate. I smile all thru security, but as soon as Yan is out of sight the tears start rolling, but that's ok, I knew it would happen. On the plane I need to relax and sleep, since thanks to two wonderful Parisians I didn't get much sleep, but I will never complain about that. The plane ride is so different than the one over to Paris, it is calm, and I could maybe call it boring. But people when I get back to my island I will be the most relaxed person in the world. Now I can go home and write a terrific, sexy story for you guys to enjoy. I just hope that I get my chance to take that vacation and meet some people to play and have fun with. If you like this you'll love the next one.

Chastity12

Out in the Cabin

Well I'm looking for someone to fulfill one of my last fantasies I have (not really last wit this dirty lil' mind of mine) and your name popped in my head. Why? Maybe, because you made reality fantasies I didn't even know I had. Plus you are as much of a sexual pervert as I am. Anyhow. Anytime. Anywhere. That's us. Maybe because, sexually we click like I've never with anyone else, even if it can never go further than just sex. This detail with you I have to remember, since I almost fell in love the last time we had our little sexcapade, now I hope I know better. This time, not my place, not yours, we're going on a trip. Where? You ask. A cabin in Yosemite National Park (California). Why? Now you just asking too many questions, but I'll answer this one question. I want a cabin with a fireplace and a big fur rug right in front of it. I also want lots of snow outside. That is my fantasy. Come on, pa. Just say yes.

Too easy! I already knew that you were going to say yes, so the tickets are already paid for, travel plans done, cabin and car rented. All you have to do is pack some clothes (not a lot, not going to be using much) just in case we need to go out. Oh, almost forgot to tell you...................... We're leaving on Thursday; your boss Ok'ed it already. Am I the bomb or what? I can't wait to have you all to myself again, even if only for a few days. I just love that sexy smile of yours; I could look at it all day, just thinking of you smiling at me like that while I have you deep in my mouth. You taste so good, I'm already wet and feenin' for you. Mira nene, go home, get your stuff ready and I'll pick you up Thursday at 11am. Be ready!

I bring breakfast on Thursday since I know there's never nothing to eat at your place and of course you slept in. At least your things are ready and by the door. We enjoy breakfast together and a quick shower (I love bathing with you). Throw everything in your trunk and close up my car to leave at your place; off we go. At the airport we seem like a couple in love, holding hands, laughing, kissing and touching. The way your body responds to me is incredible, that's one of the reasons I thought we were meant to be together. Now I know we just have a great sexual connection (plus we can talk to each other). We really have a good time together; I enjoy your company very much. I know I have you really to myself for 5 full nights, in a place where no one knows us and most importantly NO CELL PHONES, we will be completely stranded out there (don't be scared, there's other people and you'll have a T.V.). The plane ride is a bit long, but we always find something to talk about, plus we pass a lot of time kissing and touching, but no sex for you just yet, you'll get into the High Mile Club (sex in an airplane) soon enough, maybe on our way back to P.R. I want you really hot and horny when we get to the cabin. It's a fairly good trip and now we are here.

OH SHIT!!! It's so fucking cold here. Thankfully I brought a good coat and my comfy boots; you're good to go also. You fold me in your arms and I'm not cold anymore. Since we both have carry on's we get out of there pretty fast, get our car, at the rental place we get directions to Yosemite, seems easy enough, but it's already dark so we are taking our sweet time there. Tonight we just gonna chill (but you don't know that yet). Surprise! Don't worry I'll explain when we get there. It's just beautiful out here, but I'm fighting between looking out the window and staring at your gorgeous face, I could never get enough of you. I'm better off looking at the scenery. Well we get there about an hour later, pick up our keys and head to the cabin in the woods. This place has about 20 cabins, but with lots of space between each other, about 70 feet in between. More than enough so that no one can hear us during our throes of passion. We get to cabin #7, it's beautiful! Smoke is already coming out of the chimney, so I guess the fire is already burning. It has a nice wraparound porch with a swing love seat and a hammock (you know we'll be having sex there), the inside is as beautiful as the outside, I called ahead to have groceries already there, other than candles, a music station and some good wine. We put our things away and sit on the rug in front of the fireplace with some wine, just talking and unwinding from the trip, that's one of the things I most love of spending time with you (I've mentioned it already, but I am talking about you), we can just drink, talk and touch, without having to go all the way, you are my friend before anything else (unless you are really horny). Tonight it'll be about foreplay, no oral sex, no sex at all, just licking, kissing, touching everywhere except my kitty and you're delicious cock. I leave you for a bit, just the usual excuse, gonna put on something more comfortable, but the reality is I'm going to get the Jacuzzi ready for us. Hot water rose petals and lavender oil (to relax you), come back to the living room in a little, itty, bitty red negligee, you are just staring, since it's the first time you see me this way, we've never been on a real date, so you've never seen me dressed up and I've never used lingerie for you either, at least not till tonight. Tonight you are seeing me with different eyes. I walk up to you and straddle you on the floor, drink some wine from your glass and kiss you, you taste the wine on my tongue and suck it to get a better taste, you kiss my neck and shoulder, try to reach further down but not just yet. I get off you, take your hand and walk towards the bathroom. The cabin is mostly dark, except the living room cause of the fireplace and the bathroom cause of the candles; it seems like hundreds, (thanks to the mirrors) smells sweet and relaxing. You undress and expect me to also, but another surprise, I walk into the Jacuzzi with my negligee` on (done this before) sit in the water for a few seconds making sure everything is wet, put my head back in the water to also soak it and stand up. You look dumbfounded, exactly the reaction I was going for, I walk up to you, your eyes are glassed over like if you were in a trance, your hand comes to my face and you caress me with the back of it, then your fingers go to my chin, neck, shoulders, down my arm till you reach my hand, you bring my hand up to your chest and put it on top of your heart (it's both sexy and sweet but I'm not going to read anything in to this). We kiss, holding each other tight, you nude and dry, me clothed and wet. I break the kiss long enough to get you in the Jacuzzi, sponge the hot water over your head, the smells are just intoxicating, turn on the jets and sit behind you. I wash your hair while massaging your scalp, put a lot of soap on the sponge and bathe you from behind, then start rinsing your head and body with a wine glass. I have some oil and start rubbing it into your skin, pull you towards me so that at this moment your back is resting on my breasts. I'm massaging your neck and shoulders (I love touching you, your skin is so soft), then start with your arms and chest. I know you're excited, (other than seeing your delicious erection). I can feel it, by the way you tremble each time my hand glides over your skin or because of the goose bumps on them, the way you bite your lips, plus I can see the way your eyes follow my hands in the mirror. I tell you to close your eyes so I can massage your face (which is just an excuse) if you keep looking at me like that I won't be able to go thru with the no sex tonight thing, thankfully you do as I ask. I pour some warm water over your face and head, warm a bit of oil and work on your face and scalp, which works as it's supposed to, puts you to sleep; now I can relax a bit. Just having you like this, for myself, my legs wrapped around your waist and my arms on your chest, your head resting on my chest, your hands on my legs, now I'm good. I wake you 20 minutes later and only cause the water is getting cool. We take a quick shower, tell you to get comfortable in bed so I can finish the massage; one thing I can say for sure is that I know how much you enjoy me touching you, so you go jump on the bed. I take advantage that you are out of the bathroom to put on a long, see thru, white night gown. When I walked in the room your eyes almost popped out, then you blurt out "how am I supposed to relax when you keep putting on all those sexy outfits on." Just chill, boo. Take it all in since this might not ever happen again, so sshhhh. Got my oil, started rubbing it all on your back, glutes, legs, down to your feet, 25 minutes into the massage I hear you snoring (good, just sleep). I stayed up about an hour afterwards to just look at you, this way you can't read anything in my eyes, you turn over and pull me to your chest and there I fall asleep.

Mmmmm smells so good. I turn over reaching out for you, but you're not there. Open my eyes, the room is still dark but now it feels cold (not freezing). I go take a shower and put on some warm clothes, since I want to go for a walk thru the woods. As the minutes go by it smells better and better, once I get out of the bathroom I see you sitting in bed with a tray that has eggs, bacon, toast, strawberries, orange juice and coffee (never had anyone serve me breakfast) I go thru a lot of firsts with you. I sit with you and we eat from the same plate. You just have jeans on, no shirt, no shoes and the jeans aren't even buttoned, you are so fucking sexy!! I don't think there'll be a time when I look at you without wanting you. Like always you ask why I have so much clothes on, if it were for you we'd be nude all day (not that I do much complaining about it). I tell you about my plans for a walk; you think it's a great idea. I wait for you to finish dressing on the porch, just taking everything in, the only other place I've felt so at peace in a strange way, was in Kuwait. But this is much better, I'm here with you. (Would somebody please tell me why I keep doing this to myself?) Anyway. You come out looking sexy and sporty, I'm sitting on the hand banister in the corner of the porch, just looking, wishing things between us could be so different, not only sexual and more casual than just friends. But I snap out of it as soon as you look my way and smile as if you know what's going thru my mind (but that's impossible, or is it?) do you really know how deep my feelings are for you? I could actually say that I feel in love with you months ago and it just hasn't gone away. (Ahh shut up; let's go back to the good stuff). You walk up to me, stand in between my legs and hug me long and hard, give me a little kiss and say, "Let's go before I change my mind about the walk and take you right here and now." I just laugh it off, but you know I deny you nothing. You're the only man I've given myself so completely to. Our walk was breathtaking (in a good way) everything is so beautiful and clean, we really don't talk much, we just hold hands and walk, whenever you felt I was a bit out of air you'd slow down the pace a bit and kissed me. We came to a frozen pond; I had never seen one before, amazing the way nature works. We sit on a fallen tree facing each other, hand in hand and just stare: as soon as you are about to speak I shush you, I want to keep this memory forever, just like this, no words needed. A few minutes later you get up to walk around, leaving me there lost with my 1 thousand thoughts, a bit later I hear you calling my name, it sounds far away as if you were whispering it. I look up to see you shirtless on the other side of the pond, I have to laugh, sometimes you act so silly, but it's you and your crazy antics (your best feature), very sexy none the less. I walk towards you as a hypnotized person would, wasn't even feeling the cold anymore. All I wanted was to feel the warmth of your body on my hands and lips. As soon as I reach you my lips kiss your chest (mostly cause of the height difference), but what a beautiful chest it is, suck on your shoulder, nipples and your flat board stomach, your hands are in my hair for the ride. Pull me up and kiss me hard without taking your hands out of my hair, which I love. You push me against a tree and turn me to face it, your other hand on my breast while you whisper, "Lose the pants and underwear." My comeback is "what underwear?" I know you too well. Pants undone to my knees (now I can feel the cold), now both your hands are under my sweater kneading my tits, your mouth on my neck driving me crazy, then I feel you drive into me with such intensity, such passion, tears roll down my face, why? Who knows? It was just that powerful, maybe you plus the cold and the nature did it for me, but I'm almost sure you felt it too. We came in what felt like seconds. You took off our coats and put them down on the snow and loved me there once more, this time calmer, we were so in sync with our surroundings it was crazy, we were almost naked in the woods. Just then the snow started to fall, our bodies still entwined and sated, it felt magical, like everything in the world had just stopped and clicked at that exact moment. You help me up and smack my ass (the moment is gone and romance is forgotten). Start getting dressed, so we can head back. You grab my hand and we start back, this time talking all the way.

Seems we've been gone for awhile, even though we did have a late breakfast, I'd say it's about 5pm and I'm so hungry. As soon as we walk in, I start looking for something fast to cook, but you have other plans. "Let's go out to a nice restaurant, put on that little black dress you brought and baby, just dress and shoes, nothing else." You know you don't have to tell me twice. We jump in the shower together, big mistake, that was another hour. We lathered each other up, I massaged your head under the hot water while you ate my sweet chochita, then I went to my knees and took you all into my mouth. You taste so damn good, grabbed your butt while sucking you all in. I enjoy hearing you moan and know you are on the brink of cumming, so I suck you faster and harder, I want all your cum. You like when I swallow your cum, so I keep sucking that sensitive dick until you blow up in my mouth. Now I feel like going to bed, not out, but you insist on it. We get dressed and out the door. You always hold my hand or caress my thigh when you drive, I feel like I'm yours and you are all mine. How cruel is life when you can give yourself entirely to one person with no conditions and yet that person just sees you as sexual satisfaction and a friend, but knows, you are his. What are we to do?

The restaurant was nice, first it was real festive and as it gets later things wound down, the room becomes darker and the music slower. We kiss; you pull me to dance, all the while touching my body. I know you're excited already, I feel your hardness against my belly, and me, well getting wetter by the second, it's always like this with you. We decide it's time to leave; the trip back is only about 20 minutes, in which we are holding hands but very quiet. I don't even want to think, I just want to feel. We get to the cabin, out of the car and once we reach the front door, you turn around, grab me and kiss me. The kiss is rough as if you were mad, you slam me against the front door turning me to face it and pulling my dress up (Won't lie, felt scary for a bit but I was too aroused to care and it was you) You entered me hard from behind and as much as I enjoy our sex, this seemed mad, really mad, at the point where you are hurting me. Your hands are grabbing my tits so hard, you are marking my back, neck and shoulders with your bites, you are slamming into me with such force that my pubic bone is hitting the door, tears are rolling down my face (what have I done to make you want to hurt me like this?) You stop just as soon as you began, you take yourself out of me and turn me around, your eyes are red, I see sadness and now I realize why you stopped, I was sobbing, trying to control myself but can't (hiccups and all). You pull me to you in an embrace, I cower away in fear but you still hug me, promising it will never happen again (now I know how battered woman feel like, loving the men that hurt them), we stand there for a few minutes then I turn around to walk in. no words are said, I go to our bedroom and for the first time since I've known you I close the door and lock it. Shower alone. After a long, cold shower, I get the Jacuzzi going, really hot water and lots of oil and bubbles almost can't stand the heat of the water, but slowly but surely my body adjusts and I sink in, turn on the jets so they disguise the sound of my crying. I wake up with a start, the water is so cold and I hear you calling my name softly thru the door. I tell you I'll be out in a few, when I look at my watch I see I've been in here for about 3 hours, it's almost morning. What a nightmare my fantasy has turned out to be. I open the door to find you sitting next to it; you look terrible, like you haven't had a wink to sleep in the time I was in the bathroom. I sit next to you and pull your head down to my lap then start caressing it, you pull away saying you don't deserve me being so gentle towards you after what you did, I just answer "That's the way love is." You stand up, take me in your arms and walk to the bed, where you put me down softly, and then you lay with me, just holding me. "Why does this have to be so difficult?" You ask. I don't answer; just breathe in the scent of you. While your hand runs thru my hair I can't help but want you. But I can't have sex with you now, it just wouldn't feel right. I feel your body relax, guess you fell asleep. I wait about 30 minutes and get out of bed, put on shorts and a tee and walk out to the porch. Damn it's cold out here!!! But I need this, sit in the hammock with a throw that is already there and watch the beauty of nature. Sun coming up, animals waking from their slumber and the miraculous way everything look alive.

Guess I fell asleep (again). But I'm not cold anymore; the sun is shining hot on me. When I look around you are sitting on the porch steps. "I thought you left me when I woke I didn't find you in bed", you whisper more to yourself than to me, but I couldn't answer, the truth is too big, how would you react if I told you I could never leave you? So I better just leave everything as is. I get up kiss you and walk inside. Let's get cooking. After a short shower, I head to the kitchen and start cooking, you got some nice music on and some wine already served for us. After the food is all turned on, I go looking for you, find you in front of the fireplace just staring into the flames, quiet, still, just standing there. I go to you and hug you from behind, your chest feels so hard and firm under my soft hands, you take one of my hands and kiss it softly, then place it on top of your heart, "This is where you are." I'm frozen in place, but quiet. I move away, but I'll be right back, got to check on the food, you grab me and tell me we have to talk about last night and us. Please not now, let's wait till we are back in reality, we'll talk once we get to Puerto Rico, right now let's just forget about last night, let's just be who we are when we are together and flow. You let me go just saying, "whatever you want, nena." I go to the kitchen and try not to think about what was just said. You are such a complex man, I never know what to expect with you. Not physically complex, since most of the time you treat me better than anyone ever has in a long time, but emotionally, you are a different story. Dinner is ready; we eat in silence with the soft music in the background. I love looking at you; to me everything about you is amazing. After we are done eating, I go prepare us a couple of mugs of hot cocoa with marshmallows and invite out to the porch. We sit in the swing, your arm on my shoulders, my head cradled in your neck just going with the flow. After an hour or so it's too cold to stay outside so we go into the living room and sit on the rug on the floor, your back against the sofa and me between your legs, my head on your chest. You start touching my tits and I just moan you take that as a go ahead, your hand slowly snakes under my shirt and pinch my nipples while you graze my earlobe with your teeth. Now this is nice. I feel the wetness between my legs, but you already know how wet I am, because every time you play with my tits this is the reaction. You tell me to lie back on a pillow on the floor; you lie beside me and touch me so softly. Start taking off what little clothes I have on, making sure to kiss every bit of exposed skin, take a bit of extra time on my belly (U know I think I'm fat), you cherish my tummy and say I should love it more than the rest of my body, since this is where my babies lived within me. You are so great when you speak to me like that. You lick it, kiss it, suck it, my belly is getting lots of love. But you don't stop there, your hands are everywhere, while you are nibbling on my thighs your hands are on my belly. Always touching, feeling as if you can't get enough of me. You sat things into my body, whispering so softly, to me it's just a caress, if only I could understand your words, but my body just lets me feel (what I'm feeling is scary). I'm so close, yet my body is still afraid of your reaction, even though you're being so gentle. I know you sense my fear so you whisper, "its ok, we're ok, what I did before will never happen again. I need you to cum for me, nena." Just those words really help. As soon as you put your mouth on my pussy it's like a volcano erupting, fast, hot and urgent. I want you in me so bad, I beg you, urge you to put your big, thick cock all in me. But you don't, you want this to be just for me, you want me to scream your name while you savor the nectar of my love. I've cum for you before, but never like this, so raw and open, me giving myself completely to you. It's so beautiful and yet it still doesn't feel right, all because you can't let go, you can't give me you completely, you don't let me feel all of you, never all mine. Tonight I don't care, I'm just gonna continue acting like the bitch you enjoy, let it all be about me then, 2 can play this game. You keep your fingers deep inside and I keep my hips gyrating for more, just so I could feel you deeper. I lift my hips up while pushing your head down to my hot, waiting wet pussy. I want you to suck her again, I want to feel your thick tongue deep in my hole, you start pinching my nipples hard, at this point I don't know if I want your mouth on my pussy or my tits, you make the decision for me when you turn me over ass up in the air and start eating ass and pussy simultaneously. Oh Damn! Grabbing on to the rug really doesn't help much, I can already feel the pressure, it's like I haven't cum in weeks instead of mere moments ago. This is my favorite position of getting eaten out, me on all fours and you from behind and underneath. Mmmmm!!! You are too good. I cum again, it's all consuming, but you don't stop, I feel my juices dripping down my thighs and you are just licking them all up. Your mouth back on my swollen pebble and it hurts so good, I feel the ripples of my last orgasm collide with the new one. At that exact moment I smother you with my pussy, you bite, lick and suck on her so damn good. I throw myself completely on the rug, there's no way my legs can take it any longer, and I assume a fetal position, bringing my legs tight together, since the sensations of your mouth on my pussy are still assailing me. You lay behind me and there we fall asleep. How I like this nice, cozy fireplace.

Good morning, afternoon or whatever it is already. I wake up to find myself alone, covered with a throw and very sore, but it's a good kind of sore. I wrap the throw around me and get up to look for you, nada, nowhere to be seen, guess you went to town or somewhere about cause you took the car. I turn on the coffeemaker, make some toast; after I'm done with my breakfast, I grab another mug of coffee and go take a nice hot bath, really needed this. The hot water, lavender oil and the tranquility of this place knocks me out again. It seems that since we've been here our time has been divided between a lot of sleeping and more sexing. Really don't know how long I slept, but it's still quiet so you probably not back yet. Put on some running clothes and step out for a jog, really need to relax a bit, we have a lot of tension between us, emotional and sexual. After I've been out in the woods for about two hours I start back, as soon as I reach the porch I see you there on the hammock, you look so calm and collected, I don't walk up to you yet. I look at you from afar just wishing, wondering, that is until you look my way and smile. "I was getting lonely" is all you say. I go to you and lightly caress your lips with mine, you swat at my bottom on my way in. you ask if I have anything planned for today, but I don't want to do anything today, no sex, no going out, nada. I just want to chill and talk, get to know you and find out what makes you tick. You look at me as if I'd grown a second nose or something, but all you say is ok. We start on dinner while munching on a sandwich and chips. It was lots of fun, we flirted a lot, soft caresses and sweet kisses were given here and there, but nothing too deep. Sometimes I think we would be so good for each other, but this is real life. I'm a single mother with 2 teenage boys, bills coming out of my ears, you, well you are a single man with close to no responsibilities, one thing you always made clear to me was that you weren't looking for anything serious. I gave you what you wanted and took what I needed; at least that's what we thought we were doing at first. After a nice pasta dinner we sit by the fireplace, listening to music and sipping on fruity wine. Everything seems so perfect when I'm in your arms, at least here, away from the real world. You nuzzle my neck and breathe deeply, as if you were memorizing my scent. I should know since I do that and more with you, every time I touch you I close my eyes, taking in the feel of your skin, soft and silky, your hands calloused and firm, your erection, (God!) always hard and heavy on my hand. Then when I lick, kiss and suck you, (which I do a lot since I love the taste of you), I wish I could have that salty taste ingrained on my taste buds forever. When we kiss, it's like an explosion to my senses, since I get to feel and taste you, all in a kiss, your mouth is always sweet and tangy, your thick tongue playing with mine, you just don't know how much I enjoy sucking on it. I get so aroused by just the feel of your tongue in my mouth and your teeth nipping at my lips (Mmmmm), I can tell how aroused you are by our kiss also. And when you fall asleep aroused after we've had great, mind blowing sex, I lay next to you still caressing you and just taking you all in, I could definitely spend the rest of my life waking up to you in my bed or wherever we fall asleep at. Sometimes I wish I could've kept this casual, but you are just too sweet and sexual for that (how many women have fallen for your game?); I feel for your tricks, I fell in love with the man. It's incredible to see how comfortable we are with each other, no words are needed when we are together, and everything just flows. We fall asleep in each other's arms.

This morning is beautiful; we take a quick shower together, light breakfast and take a stroll in the woods. We decide to have a late lunch at a quaint little restaurant, great view, delicious food, we were there for about 3 or 4 hours, just enjoying the scenery and each other's company. As we walk back you take my hand in yours and stop by the pond where we made love days before, you look so serious. "We really need to talk about us, about all this happening between us. I seriously can't imagine going back and not having you in the same house or in my bed. this has become more than sex and I know you feel the same, during the day I think about how you are and what you're doing, if you're thinking of me, if you miss me as much as I you." I interrupt, just to shut you up, really can't believe you are saying all these things to me. "Please let me finish, it's important", you say. I look away but you grab my face to look at you. "Please don't look away and listen carefully to what I'm saying. When I have to go to bed at night without you, all I think about is how your naked body fits mine so well, how good it feels to touch your soft as silk skin, but most of all how good it feels to be buried deep inside you, but let me make this clear, it's not all because of the sex, it's the connection that I feel at that moment with you, it's as if nothing else exists, just us. You make me feel alive." Tears are just flowing like a river down my face, I kiss you, pull you back to the cabin. It's already getting dark on our last night here. We come in to the cabin, almost ripping our clothes off, but we go all the way into the room, there I push you on the bed and knell on top of you. I kiss, bite and lick you, all the time your hands on my ass, moving slowly up to my head, where you grab me by the hair and pull so you have better access to my neck. I can feel your big hard cock throbbing underneath me, I do know how much you want me, maybe you even need me, and tonight you will be getting all of me

(Again). I make love to you thoroughly, nothing is left without being licked, kissed or bitten, and I give you my ass, mouth and pussy to use as you wish. After we make love for over 3 hours, we take a warm bath in the Jacuzzi and there we make love once again and afterwards I bathe you, give you a massage with warm vanilla oil. You fall asleep under my hands; I can feel your breathing get deeper slower. I put on one of your shirts, turn away from you and cry till I fall asleep.

We wake up early since we have to be leaving before noon, you prepare breakfast while I take a quick shower, then we eat together, you're all lovey dovey this morning, I'm being myself. We pack everything into the car and head to the airport. We take the car to the rental place and go to catch our plane, where I will make you a VIP to the Mile High Club. I am a woman of my word, I said on our trip back and here we go. After I take care of you, you sleep like a baby and I just stay up thinking about what I'm going to do as soon as we get back. As the plane lands I know what I have to do. You grab my hand as we start towards the door and out to the ramp, still have a tight hold when we get to the luggage carousel. We get you truck and on our way to your place we make a quick stop for some food to go, we reach your place, put my luggage in my car, eat and since I'm staying the night we take a shower and lay down to watch a movie, we both fall asleep. At about 3am I wake up, kiss you softly so you don't wake, whisper a good-bye into your hair and tiptoe out the room and down to my car. Make sure not to make a lot of noise as I leave and make sure to turn off my cell, I can't talk to you right now, and you may have me turning around and back to your bed. I'm glad in a way that you never went to my home, now you don't know where to find me at, my cell number I can always change or met my children, don't have to give out to many explanations. Might be asking why am I leaving now that you told me how you feel, easy, not once did you say you loved me or spoke about my children and that was a real big deal breaker. Like I said in a fantasy world it's just you and me, in reality, it's a lot of people we have to deal with, not only our families, but also our coworkers. I really don't think you would've coped well with that type of situation. And I can't be with you like that. As much as I thought my love could be enough for both of us, I found out otherwise, I can only love so much. Not every story has a happy ending, I really wanted this to work, not just for me, but for both of us, many time I've mentioned how good we are for each other and together, and in my heart I know we could've been so happy if the cards would've been dealt differently.

But on a lighter note, my fantasy was brought to reality, you will always be my fantasy man, the man I dream of but will never have for myself. Who knows? Maybe the future holds many more fantasies for us to bring to life together or maybe this was our last, but until you figure out what you really want for yourself we can never be together. Always remember I am here for you whenever you need me, not only as a lover but as a friend. I just ask you to give me some time to regroup and get my feeling in order; many in a few months I can be that sexy vixen you like to sex so much. This is only for the best. I'll be in touch

Chastity 13

My Military Secret

Have you ever fantasized about being with someone in the military? If you haven't, you don't know what you're missing, if you've been with a service member, you know what I'm thinking about and you still want so much more.

Well me, I'm on both sides of that coin. Not saying all military personnel know what they're doing in the sack, I've met some lousy ones (no names), but my greatest lovers have been in the military, one being a sailor, the other a soldier. The best ever in my life! (At least till this was written) Oh MY!!! Even thinking about it gets me worked up still. I'm not going to say I'm the best you'll ever have, but I'm sure up there and I am in the Army. You get to learn a lot of tricks around the way, so many guys talking about what they like and dislike during sex, in a relationship and if what is going on is indeed a relationship.

Let's get back to the fantasies, people.................................

Uniforms! Uniforms! What woman can pass by a Marine in his Dress Blues and not look twice or maybe a Police Officer with a booming body or perhaps one of my fellow soldiers in their DCU's? I know I can't. Let me tell you from experience not everyone looks good in uniform, but those that do.......... Help me God!

Just think about this:

It's a sunny day in September, just how I like them. I love that you can feel the trees come to life; see the different colors of the leaves, the bite of cold in the nice breeze in autumn. (That's why I picked this time of the year). I'm just strolling down the street in this beautiful military installation, in my short jean skirt (love my legs), nice t-shirt that shows off my tits, a cute hat and sneakers. So many men to pick from to play with and so little time to do so. Just then, the aura of you sucks me in.

it's like you are golden, all around you specks of gold light, nice, the sun is exactly behind you, almost blinding me but I still can't look away. You seem to be so comfortable in this environment; the uniform fits perfectly, not tight and not too baggy, just right. I had to stop then and there and just stare at you. At that exact moment, I guess you feel the power of my intense scrutinizing stare; you look towards me and God! You smile, if I thought you were good looking before the smile, after it you became gorgeous. A minute later you jump off the truck you were working on, come walking straight towards me, making me feel a bit anxious and nervous, a big first for me, since I'm usually the predator and not the prey and at this moment I feel like prey big time. The way you look at me is mesmerizing, almost hypnotic; my eyes are glued to yours, but once I'm able to blink you are right in front of me, with that beautiful, sexy smile. As a whole you are stunning, eyes that draw you in, a smile that is just perfect in every way and your body, damn, not even a Greek God can compare (and this with your clothes on, can't wait to take them all off). You say hi and I was just lost for words, which is very uncommon, I was just openly staring. You laughed and my blood pressure sky rocketed, such a sensual sound, you turn around, make some muscle poses sticking out that curvy, firm butt, but my eyes are concentrating on your broad, wide back and hard arms. You swiftly turn back and asked me if that was sufficient for me or if I wanted to continue observing. I smile, tilt my head to the side for effect and just say, "Pa, for me that was just an appetizer, I'm waiting for the main course." And there you go again, that fascinating laugh and shoot back, "For someone without a voice a few minutes ago, that was a great comeback." You should know that is just the start for me.

We had lunch together, and then you had to get back to work, so we made plans for this evening. We met up at a club outside the base, it's a nice, cozy place, I've been here before, but tonight it'll become my playground. I made sure to be there before you arrived, wanted to be seen in my tight, short, little outfit. Men wanted to be near me, some cute sailor bought me a drink after a sexy dance. I sat where I could see you before you saw me when you got there. I wasn't expecting what I saw, you looked striking, and I've never seen such a magnificent specimen of a man in my life. You look good in uniform but in civi's you look just delicious. You walk around the club a bit once you get there, that's till one of my friends points me out, you look from afar, just taking me in, looking at the way other men are staring at me and just thinking of ways of playing with that. You walk towards me confident. I felt like I was being stalked by a big cat, your eyes seem to glow in the dark, your body sinuously flowing my way, a sexy smirk on those beautiful lips. I was enthralled by you as a whole. I stood to greet you and your arms came around me, grabbing my ass hard, pulling me towards you, then you just stare into my eyes, daring me to take what I want, since you already made the first moves. (You'll get to know not to dare me) I stand on my tip toes, grab your face and pull you even closer for a luscious, long kiss. Mmmmm I can feel your dick getting hard as I rub my pelvis on you. This is so exciting, you feel so good. One thing is for sure, you can definitely kiss, and I could spend the whole night just kissing you, but I'm so sure it would lead to many other yummy activities. Kissing you is like sucking on ones favorite piece of candy, you suck on it like you just can't get enough but then you slow down cause you don't want it to finish. I pull away because if I don't we'd be doing some freaky shit right here and now, you are very tempting, my love. You take a step back and just openly admire me, step back into my space and there you stay. Caressing my legs, saying how beautiful I am, touching all of me like no one else existed around us. You make me feel beautiful, desired, sexy and very much wanted. Men and women alike were staring, men, well I always wear sexy clothes and I am attractive; women, what can I say, you are the epiphany of tall, dark and handsome, plus you have this sexiness about yourself that even makes you seem conceited at times. But I know you're not. We dance a few songs, but between that and your kisses I just wanna take you to bed right now. Didn't have to tell you twice.......... So to bed it is, it was all so sultry and sexy, everything was perfect, well except that we were missing some matches for the candles I had brought, some of them became hot oil for massages, but you made up for that many times over. The first time we came together wasn't even on the bed, it was in the shower, (remind me never to get my hair blow-dried before a date or outing with you), but you sure won't hear me complaining about my hair getting wet. Under the warm water, after you bathed me completely, caressing every little part of my body as if I was the most fragile piece of art, as if I were priceless. Once we get to the bed, gloves come off, it was an all goes fuck fest, you're a big boy (all around), but I'm also a big girl who knows how to handle her man and baby I will handle you as many times as you let me, (really hope we have many, many times together). God you can really kiss, don't even need the sex, but don't get me wrong I do want it, very much so. Everything was just faultless (except for the damn matches). It's almost time to go but I need to have me a real good taste of you, so I can savor it till our next time. So I lay you back and take out my secret weapon, a little man vibrator that goes right on your penis. At first you don't want it near you, but at last I convince you and what a ride it is. All for you, my pleasure is looking at your face while you fight back your orgasm, but I take it a step further when I suck your crown, lick around that yummy, big, cock while stroking it and our little toy at work. After about 30-45 minutes of this, the little vibrator starts to die, but I keep sucking on my new favorite chocolate candy, until you push me away just so you can pull me towards you and give you better access to my hot, wet, waiting pussy. Push all your huge cock in me at once, it hurts a bit, but the pain is well worth all the pleasure I feel with you in me, on me. You still don't cum, it takes a bit more fun and lots more kisses, but when you do orgasm it's so explosive; at that moment I feel the need to pull you in so much more deeper than you already are, the need to be one with you is overwhelming. I have the feeling that you will become a very important person in my life, you give me a vibe of as much. I'm already hoping that this is more than just a fling. We lay there exhausted, but I stare fascinated at the mirrors above the bed, you on top of me, our bodies still melded together, legs entwined. I love the way our skin colors look so perfect together, you being so dark and I so fair. I would love to fall asleep like this every night, but I know better than to wish for anything. I will just be satisfied with whatever I can have of your striking body, magnificent love making and of course more of those delectable kisses. But at the end of the night we have to say our good byes and just hope that our next time is sooner rather than later. I have so much more in mind for you my beautiful, dark skinned soldier. So much more..........

Chastity14

Girls or Women????

Well my friends it's time to school you on the facts of life. Men think they're so slick when they leave us, beautiful, mature women, for little girls that are only interested in what they can obtain from them, that, mostly being money. We, on the other hand (or at least ME!) know, two can play this game, so now I keep my eye out on sweet, young studs, which enjoy very much the sexy tricks we older gals know so well. I for one, don't keep a man (financially speaking), everything is 50/50 or better yet, just sexual. I really love me a hard, firm, long lasting dick, and let me tell you, most of them just want to be in your good graces, so they can keep getting some of that aged, but very delicious pussy, so you know they will do their best to keep you satisfied in and out of the bedroom. And in my opinion that is an absolute 10. That man will treat you as a queen when he has you and day dream of all the different, new things to do to you while you're apart. Then there's the thing of them being like the Energizer Bunny, they keep going and going and going (for real, they do!) And it's not just bust a nut and we done, oh no, they cum and we just get to start everything all over again and again and again. It's like having your own personal trainer, cause let me tell you, that's a full work out and then some.

Everything is so different and more so if the age difference is far and apart. Guys, do you even know how good it feels to be looked at as if they wanted to eat you? As if they didn't have you right then and there they would die? Well that's how younger men look at us older gals, some older guys too (when they knows what's up), but mostly the older gentlemen take us for granted as if we will always be there just in case their little girls leave their asses when they're straight broke, well no more!! We're not to be treated like scraps on your plate, when we know in our hearts that we are and always will be the main dish. Being with a younger man is a risk, but nowadays taking a breath is a risk, taking risks is what being alive is all about, if you take risks you'll never have to ask yourself what if? Me, personally, I try everything I can at least once, be it, cooking, eating, dressing and most of all sexually, don't kick it till you try it and if you enjoy it keep doing it until you perfect it. What is better than doing something you enjoy? Doing it better than anyone else. Men, (of any age) love it when you know what you're doing to them, having confidence in your skills is such a turn on. And girls, even when you don't know what the hell you are doing, don't let them in on that!

Another reason why us mature, sexy women have so much fun in the bedroom, is that, be it with older or younger men we always are very open sexually and have miles of confidence to boot. Men any age would rather be with a woman that knows what she wants, when she wants it and if it's not given or offered to us, we just go get it. Sometimes young chicks think that just by flaunting their bodies around is enough to get any mans engine going, but maybe the body gets them started but if there's no gas to keep that engine going, it all ends there. It doesn't always work with just glam, a man needs someone they can speak with, someone who can understand what they're going thru in the real adult world, a woman who isn't afraid to tell them to hit that pussy hard or grab on your dick out in the open, cause if it's mine, it's mine. He'll probably be embarrassed for a quick minute, but after that has passed he will be too excited to give a damn. This is me, and ladies, my advice, all of us should have that little, sexy vixen come out of us from time to time, the more often the better. She does wonders for our love life. Be naughty but always safe..........................

Chastity 15

Gone

I've been thinking about this 1 for a while, since you know I do a lot of traveling. It's kind of weird, but you guys should know that I can't be monotonous in my writing, so I wanted to do something different. This one is more romantic then sexy, but the sexiness is always there.

I'm still tripping on if this was all a dream or if any of it really happened, even though I shouldn't be with all the proof I have of this reality. Let me tell you all about it.

It all started on a balmy rainy night in May, I was home all by myself (not surprised about that). For a few days, I've been having this strange feeling, as if I was being watched, but really didn't pay any mind to it, but tonight it was different, maybe I'm just being paranoid or something, but I felt someone looking at me or worst thru me, almost reaching out to touch me. I've been feeling eager to get home all day, I get home take a really cold shower and lay down on the sofa to watch a bit of television while I sip on some fruity wine. There's this sweet aroma in the air, I just can't pinpoint what it is, but it's so sweet. My eyes feel so heavy all of the sudden, my mouth is dry, I reach out to grab my phone, but a hand snaps it up before mine, I look up but even my vision is blurry and anyways…. Who's the owner of that hand? ………. No more ………… Guess I'm out for now.

I start hearing stuff again, but I'm soooo sleepy, my eyes just will not open, I must be mumbling or something not saying much, but it was enough for whomever to stick me in the arm with whatever is keeping me sleeeeppyy ………………………. Out once again. Who knows for how long I've been out, I'm guessing too long, my head is killing me and I'm feeling up to opening my eyes now (Oh Shit) bad idea. Everything is black, I'm blindfolded, as I try to take it off I find that I'm also tied up, feet and hands. What the hell! I think it's time to begin to panic, I try to scream but my throat is too dry. But it keeps getting worse; I feel the bed give way beside me. God please help me! Is all I can think at this precise moment. Whoever is there caresses my cheek, I flinch at the touch, I can feel the warm breath by my ear and all that is said is, "I would never in all eternity hurt you my Queen." The voice unknown, the accent beautiful, his English perfect. Who are you? What do you want of me? Where am I? "One question at a time love, my name is Kiumee, I want you and where you are is of no significance to you at this moment." I'm so confused, is this all a nightmare or have I really been abducted? My family, my kids, my job, are they looking for me, wondering where I am. As if reading my mind, he tells me, "Everyone thinks you are on a special mission, orders were given to specific people and you're all mine for the time being." Now I was really worried, everyone thought I was ok, no one is looking for me, I'm being kept hostage God knows where by someone with that amount of power. I just started bawling like a baby then, I couldn't help myself. Kiumee picked me up from the bed as if I weighed nothing and sat me on his lap, at first I was really uncomfortable since I don't know who this man is, and I am still blindfolded and tied up, but he is so soothing, he put my head to his shoulder, caressed my hair while telling me, "Please don't be sad, I hate seeing you cry as if this was a bad thing, I only want to give you everything you ever wanted and so much more." I'm so close to him now, his scent is peculiar (he smells sexy, is that weird or what?) I think I'm going mad. After about 20 minutes in silence, he puts me on the bed and tells me he has to go but will be back soon. I don't hear him walk out or anybody walk in, but I feel a warm hand untying my legs, then my hands, I get the courage to take the blindfold off and there is a young girl shyly looking at me with interest. I started babbling, she looks confused, then starts shushing me, looking as if about to cry, I automatically shut up, she becomes calm again, but now is about to leave, she stops dead in her tracks when I stand up. In very broken English she states, "He love you very much, very good." Now I'm really lost, she pulls me toward the open balcony windows; there is beach for miles with mind blowing white sand and the bluest water I've ever seen. There is a rocky part where one lone soul sat, it seemed as if he was staring directly at me, the person was too far to capture any details other than the dark, long hair flowing in the wind and the beautiful tanned brown skin. I look at the girl and ask her if he is the one who has me captive, she lowers her eyes to the floor and just whispers, "He love you so." What's his name? I ask. Her eyes wide in surprise, "You do not know? He is our leader, Kiumee Tafari." Now she was looking at me strange as if I should've known this information, the word leader swirling in my head, and leader of what? A cult? A Looney farm? What? So many questions. I know I have to take advantage of this girl to get my questions answered. So I begin, what's your name? Do you live here? How old are you? Where is here? The first thing she answered was the last question and after that I really didn't hear any much else clearly, she said, "We are in Casablanca, silly. My name is Dikeledi, I 16; I stay here when told to." Did she really mean Casablanca as in "AFRICA"? Oh my God! Now I'm really hyperventilating , she runs screaming from the room and in come like 20 people, thank goodness one very American looking doctor comes in with the commotion, (How do I know he's a Dr? He's stethoscope gave him away) he tells me to start breathing, slowly and count from 20 back, I begin to calm down, but still, Africa!!!! I ask for Kiumee, everyone just stares as if I've gone crazy, but almost at once I hear the silky voice that had lulled me earlier, but this time it was in a language I could not understand and the voice was not soft, but hard and commanding, the people in the room started to scatter and leave before he had even entered the room, only the Dr stayed where he was. He was smiling when he walked in, and once again I found myself not breathing for a few seconds. "What a commotion you have made my beautiful princess in just a few hours of being awake." I walk towards him, stand toe to toe, definitely have to look up and what a mistake that was, I was staring into the sexiest black eyes I'd ever seen, but I was still mad as hell, I want to go home, I need to go home now, Kiumee! "I'm sorry, but not possible at this moment. Will you take a stroll on the beach with me please?" He didn't even wait for a reply, he took my hand and pulled me away; the Dr smiled, I just wanted to start crying all over again. Once we started walking, he started talking. He's 39 years of age and doesn't look a day over 25, single, no children, mother is only living parent and has 2 sisters, making him the only male and he's the youngest. Another thing I noticed is that I can't take my eyes off of him, this is a man who has kidnapped me, that has taken me away from my (boring) life and I am staring as a starving puppy stares at a steak. And yet this place seems like déjà vu, as if this was my life at some point, as if I've always belonged here. Just then, his lips on mine, hungry, wanting, and who would think? I respond greedily as if always waiting for this moment. The kiss goes on, seems like hours, but not really. We are rolling in the wet sand, just as I've seen myself doing it before in my dreams or fantasies, the water caressing my body, I can feel the foam of the waves in my hair, it's all so warm, so inviting. All of the sudden I'm on my feet at arm's length and all he repeats over and over is "Not like this."

A week has passed; he has stayed away, only seeing him at meals. I'm anxious about not knowing what's going on at home, but also about why's he's kept away after bringing me half way around the world to have me. I can't take all this silence anymore, so I grab my wine, get up from the table and just walk up the stairs to the terrace on the roof, I heard everyone at the table gasp in horror, but whatever. This terrace has been my haven since I found it, looking out to the sea, swimming laps or in the Jacuzzi, just eager for him to join me at some point, should've known better since I've never been very lucky in the game of love. Anytime I was in the terrace I was totally left alone, guards at the doors but not once spoke to me or came in, if I needed anything Dikeledi was promptly sent. Since I was always alone here I got into a habit of swimming naked, so now, I slipped out of the lovely red, silk dress and dived in only my tiny, red bikini bottom. I tried to stay under water for as long as I could, thinking that maybe I would wake back home or just drown here (mostly of loneliness). About 10 seconds under water and I felt it give, when I opened my eyes it was him coming straight for me, at the surprise of it all, I took in water but made my way to the surface sputtering everywhere. I jumped out of the pool and started cussing at him in English and Spanish, he was looking as if he was mad at me. Still in the pool, but a tiny smile curling on his delicious mouth, as I followed his eyes, I remembered I was all but naked, quickly jumping back into the water. His arms came tightly around me, he whispered angrily in my ear, "Are you so sad here that you'd rather take your own life? Don't you know that I'd rather lose you to your family and your Island, knowing you are well, then lose you forever." I just stared at him and started laughing, "What's so funny?" He asks. You still have your clothes on, even your shoes. You look so funny! "But you look so beautiful with that smile upon your face." he says. Look, I would never harm myself intentionally, I have 2 handsome young men waiting for me at home to think of and to answer your question, I do miss my family very much, I'm so lonely here, always by myself; even though I was kidnapped, I've had a nice time here, but I would really like knowing why and in reality by whom. At that moment he looked so sad, I felt like I hurt his feelings, his response, "Tonight everything will be revealed to you, now, let me take off all these ruined clothes, so we can spend some leisurely time together. Would you like to wear my shirt? Even though I wish you didn't." This man is so confusing, I feel as if I'm going mad. I want the shirt, even if you can see my body thru it anyways, something is something (and I do think it's sexier this way). I wish I knew what's going thru his mind, each time I catch him looking at me, I see longing, want, sometime even sadness, but always love or tenderness. But why? We don't even know one another. He gives me the shirt and I swam a few laps, while he just sits on the side of the pool staring. As soon as I stop swimming he starts talking, "I wish so you didn't want to go away from me, you've been the center of my being for so many years, keeping you safe, loving you from afar, seeing you hurt because of men so below you; crying in silence because of your pain. That is love my princess, I want to shower you with all I am and give you all I have, this house, all my land, anything and everything you might want or need is at your disposition. I love you as many stars are in the sky, as many grains of sand are at the beach. You are my sun during the day and my moon in the evening. My love is so grand that I would rather be dirt poor and have you, then have this kingdom and live without you. You are my World, my Universe; every breath I take is in unison with yours. You complete me; I am only half a man without you in my life. I know this is a surprise for you, I'm very sorry for the way I conducted our meeting, I was just so afraid you would deny me the grace of your company and I couldn't risk that, my lovely. I beg your forgiveness for the hurt and sadness I have brought upon you." He jumped in the water and pulls me to him, until that moment I hadn't even noticed that I was crying like a baby and couldn't stop. No one ever had spoken of me with such devotion, love and strength. At this moment I feel like the most loved, cherished, wanted woman, and all this by a man who I know nothing of, other that he is the sexist thing breathing on this Earth. I know his name and this great love he professes he has for me. He held me as if I was a child and let me cry; all the while apologizing for what he'd done. God I wanted so badly to be able to catch my breath and explain my tears to this wonderful man, but all I could do was the second best thing. I pulled his face to me, looked into those beautiful, soulful eyes and just said, Thank you, but if you would just shut up and kiss me I'd feel so much better. That was all he needed. The force of his kiss surprises me if only for a moment, God this man is so passionate! My hands caress his neck and sneaks into grab all that silky hair, his hands roam my body as if it has always belonged to him and only him, he knows how and where to touch me. Unbuttons the shirt to reveal my breasts, his mouth makes a sizzling trail down my throat, my shoulder, he stops at my chest, where he tenderly kisses my butterfly and suckles the rest of the way down to my aching, waiting nipple, it's electrifying. I arch my back to give him better access, but he decides to return to my mouth, which in reality is not a problem at all. After a few minutes of exhilarating kisses, he whispers in my ear, "My Queen we must stop, please do not pout. All will be yours by nightfall, like I said before, not like this. You are too special to just sex you in the pool as our first time. I promise you, it will be worth the wait, I have a surprise for you tonight. But I do have a few questions for you to answer at this moment. Will you have me as the man in your life? As the man that will always love you above everything else except our God? As the one who will cherish you and your children until the end of our days? Will you honor me and my people by becoming my wife, my queen?" I bet I look silly now, my mouth is hanging open and I'm just dumbfounded. At last I find my voice, Kiumee I don't even know you, this is crazy, and you are crazy. You don't know who I am, the things I've done. How can you love a woman so unconditionally without knowing her? What is so special about me that you would pick me out of an array of beautiful women I bet you have at your feet? I am just a simple American single mother, with not much to offer other than my body ad even that is common and unperfected. And that you could've had a few minutes ago without a proposal. "My love, you are everything except simple. Your past? I know many things of it, but do not care; I'm more interested and want your now and our future. About the women I could have, it is true, I could have my pick out of thousands, but none were you. And about knowing you, maybe I know you better than anyone. Your feelings are so pure and strong, all of them! You feel everything 3 times stronger. When you are mad the world knows, it is etched on your face and you are not one to hold in your anger, you blow up, but not at everyone, only the persons who fueled this anger in you. When you are sad, it's a feeling you think belongs to only you, you cry in silence and always alone, you protect everyone from your sadness, but then carry it all by yourself. So many people have disappointed you over the years, your family, your so called friends, the men who've promised to care and love you, but you are an actress, you shake it off as if of no importance while facing them, but deep down you hurt. You are the best friend to all, but feel you have only a handful of people who would really be there in your time of need. But most important than anything, is the way you love. So completely, so giving, so unconditionally. You love your children like a lioness her cubs, no one will ever hurt them while you exist, you would rather starve to death than them ever feel the pangs of hunger. You would take a bullet, a knife in the heart, any type of danger or pain for them, rather you 100 times over than them, because they are yours, they came from within you and without them you would just cease to exist. Your family is important to you, there's not much you wouldn't do for them, even if this does not go both ways." I have to interrupt him, how do you know all of this? I've never seen you before my arrival here. "Shhh, I told you I do know you, for years I've been keeping track of you, since I first laid eyes on you at the airport in Kuwait, but that story I will tell you another day. You wanted to know and I am telling you, at least what I can for now. About your body, true it may not be the most perfect body, for you. But I love the curve of your hips, the little belly that you've had since having your children, the pale color of your skin that would contrast perfectly against my dark skin. You have the most perfect legs I have ever seen on a woman in my entire life and we shouldn't talk of your delicious breasts. But love, you offer me so much more than only your luscious body, you are smart, book and streets, you listen almost as much as you talk, you are compassionate, fair, loving, you keep me on my toes with your many emotions, especially when you become this sex goddess." Oh God this man is definitely mad! "Stop laughing, you do, don't think I've seen your pictures on the internet? You are a divine mix of a sexy devil and the lovely Aphrodite. But enough with all this, we should get out of here and get ready. Still I need to know, will you become my queen?" I don't know what to say, he's given reason on top of reason to say yes and I am tired of being lonely, of all the sex with no love or just love from me, of getting hurt time after time by men who don't know what they want and here I have a man offering me the world on a pedestal, plus he is gorgeous. But still I think it's too damn fast, the man is sexy, educated, seems caring, sweet and tender, but how do I know for sure? Why don't we take it slow and have a friendship with benefits (as long as I'm having sex with this man who has the looks of a God, I'm good), then get engaged and somewhere down the road then get married. He's quick to respond to my question. "My love, I know since the day I first saw you that I wanted you for my wife, at that moment I knew I had at last found my soul mate. But as fate goes, I need to know right now if you accept my proposal, before all the festivities commence. I promise to be the most loving, faithful mate to you and a dear friend to your children. Please give us this, you deserve the best and I assure you, that is me. I never want to see another tear fall from your eyes again, unless it's from happiness. My beautiful Chastity, will you accept to be my Queen, please?" I am so tired of fighting this, what's the worst that can happen? Me being unhappy, been there, done that, got a few t-shirts, and definitely will not stand for it again. Always wanted to get married, so why not do it. Kiumee, it would be an honor to call you my husband. He grabs me in a bear hug and starts screaming, "She said yes!" The guards come rushing, in a frenzy, he's laughing, but making sure to not let me go so they can't see my almost naked body, they stop in their tracks and just smile. He looks up at them and says, "Let the celebrations begin."

Everyone is going crazy. What a commotion! I was rushed off to my suites to encounter the biggest surprise since I arrived here, my family was all here; dad, mom, grandma, uncle, my brothers and most importantly my children. Everyone was excited about being brought all the way to Africa in a private jet, talking about the festivities, how beautiful everything is, and of course asking why they were all here. Well their guess is as good as mine. My dad pulled me aside; we walked out to the balcony to have some privacy. I tried to explain everything without making Kiumee out to be the bad guy, but as soon as I said that I was drugged and taken from my house, my dad had a fit, trying to calm him down, I finished explaining everything until the point where I walked in and found them there. He was still paranoid about it, but what can I say, he's my dad. Should of heard them when I told them I had agreed to marry him, they thought he'd brain washed me or I had just gone crazy. Right then about 20 people walk into the room with a whole lot of hangers and trunks, filled with clothes and shoes, for men, women, and children, all colors and sizes, different styles and colors, plus tailors to fix up whatever you liked to fit you. When I was about to pick up a beautiful satin, lavender dress, one of the people that had entered the room snapped it out of my reach, pointed to a walk in closet and said "For you." I walked over and the closet was almost as big as half my house and the biggest catch of all, it all fit me, clothing, shoes, hats, everything fit me, and all my style, a few too dressy but I may need them now. And there hanging in the middle of my room was the dress I always dreamed about getting married in. I started crying so hard, everyone came over to see what the problem was, but I was crying with a huge smile on my face. My mom just looked at me and hugged me, a real hug from my mom, and then she just said she was so happy to be here and be able to share this with me. I had to let her know, mom you've been there for my children's births and it's only fitting that you be here when at last I marry a man who loves me and wants me, flaws and all. The room became silent all of the sudden, except for my relatives. I just knew it was him, I let go of my mom and ran straight into him, kissed him as if we were the only ones in the room, my brothers started hooting as if they were at a football game and my dad cleared his throat, reminding me where I was and who were there. Kiumee introduces himself to everyone and apologizes for the way things were done. He then walks straight to my children, I freeze, instinct more than fright, but I should trust my fiancée more, he approaches my oldest and asks for his permission to marry me, my son just asks him, "Can you make my mother happy? Will you make her smile more often? Will you please make sure she doesn't cry anymore? I think she's cried enough for one lifetime. Can you do this?" Kiumee smiles at him, then looks at me, while he says, "I can surely do all the things that you ask of me and so much more. I promise to keep your mom well loved and love you guys also, my prince. This is my promise to you and with this gift I seal it." With that, he puts on my son's neck a precious multicolored gold chain with a clear diamond (which is my son's birthstone). Kiumee turns his eyes toward my youngest son and asks him, "What about you, young one. Are you ok with me marrying into your beautiful family?" My son thought for a few minutes and just asked, "Do we have to live all the way over here?" Kiumee laughed, that sexy, rich laugh and replied, "Only sometime out of the year and only if you want to be here, nothing will be too sudden or against your will. Your mother decides how all living arrangements will be worked out, even if it means not living together all year. Is that all you ask?" My youngest nods in response, Kiumee has the same kind of chain he put on my oldest, but the difference is the stone, a beautiful, cloudless peridot (which, what a surprise, is his birthstone). He gave each one of my family members a jewel as a gift, all their birth months (I was so impressed! Imagine them). And to think I don't even have an engagement ring yet. He sealed it with my mother when he walked up to her and said, "I hope your daughter is as beautiful as you are at your age." Kissing her hand and placing an amazing peridot bracelet on her wrist. He pulls me with him and he then kneels in front of my sitting grandmother, and very quietly whispers for her ears (and mine) only, "Thank you for always taking care of my beloved. I know you did it out of love, but I feel as if I owe you my life. And since I know jewelry is really of no meaning to you, I have a special gift. When you get home, you will owe nothing, everything will be paid for and whatever you ever may need, I will make sure you receive." She just kisses his cheek and tells me, "Esto era lo que tu necesitabas." Kiumee guides me to the middle of the room and asks for a minute of everyone's time. "Now all this has a reason behind it and we will just get to it at this moment. I want to officially ask this beautiful, sexy woman in front of her family, to make me the luckiest and proudest man on this earth by being my queen." He kneeled in front of me and presented me with a mind blowing diamond and ruby band, it sparkled so much I felt dizzy, but not enough to not answer the man, which I did with a whispered yes. He bowed his head, while putting on a beautiful diamond, peridot and ruby anklet on my leg, saying "This is now my life." Stood, kissed me hard and left saying, "We should get ready for our wedding unless you want to wear what you have on." WHAT! Seems like I'm getting married tonight.

Everything was a blur after that, the next time I saw myself in the mirror, I was in the gorgeous gown, everyone just staring. My father came up to me from behind, I could see our reflection, teary eyed whispered in my ear, "You are the most beautiful bride I have ever seen in my entire life, my Booboo. I just hope this rush-rush wedding doesn't lead to heartbreak. I really wish you true love and never ending happiness." He kisses my cheek and steps back. Dikeledi comes in to let us know it is time. My father and brothers walk behind me, while my children are to give me away to my groom, my grandmother and mother are my matrons of honor. When we start walking down the aisle, I can't believe the amount of people here, the room was totally packed. The music is a sweet melody played with violins, all the sudden everything is silent and someone starts announcing us, my mind went still when the person said, "Welcome all to the grand wedding of Prince Kiumee Tafari and his soon to be Princess." (OH MY GOD!!!!) I was about to turn back when he ran down to me and took me by the hands. "Please forgive me for this surprise, but it was the only way. I had only till today to pick a bride myself or my people would do it for me on the day after my 40th birthday. I needed to know you wanted me for me, not for my position or what I could offer you and yours. I want someone who will cherish, love and honor me, like I will her. I've told you many times over that I fell in love with you a long time ago and our time together here just made it stronger and much more real. Please tell me this doesn't change anything, I am still the same man I was a few hours ago, just a little bit more powerful." This said with a sad smile on his face. I was at a loss for words, what was I to do? But when I looked in his eyes I knew, this is the man I wasn't going to be able to live without, not now, when I've just found him (or better said, he kidnapped me). But however it was, we came together at last, the person that was put on this Earth specifically for me. I grab his face and kiss his lips and without losing that contact, whisper into his mouth, what are we waiting for? I thought you wanted me to be your wife? He twirled me around and before setting me on my feet again, whispers in my ear, "My life with you is bound to be full of beautiful surprises, now let's get this done with so I can I have you all to myself for at least a few hours." We start kissing again, that's until his mother comes up and asks if we could maybe wait till they finish marrying us. We look around and everybody is smiling, he takes my hand and we walk together to our destiny.

Everything went beautifully, my tiara was made of diamonds and rubies, my new husband is very detail oriented. The reception area was comfortable and elegantly decorated. Never in a thousand years did I expect something so big to happen to me. Our families sat together and talked about us as children and adults. We danced, laughed and mingled but always hand in hand, when it was about time to leave; my sons gave me a gift and told me not to open until later. I knew this had something to do with Kiumee, since they didn't know they were coming to a wedding. We walk up to the terrace where I spent most of my alone time and it was just spectacular, no lights, there were candles and rose petals of every color you can imagine a rose everywhere. I took off my shoes and it felt like walking on velvet. Everything was perfect, the bed is on a platform in the middle of the pool, to get there, he had put what seemed like stepping stones, in the water, there was water lilies and floating candles, just enough to not be too much. The bed also had petals, but those were lilac colored, because he knew this is my favorite color. My mouth was wide open; I couldn't believe all this was for me. He took my hand and together we walked as if on water toward the beautifully laid out bed, once there, he gently places me atop the petals, stares a few minutes, raises his eyes to the skies and says a few phrases in his own language. I'm still dumbfounded by everything. That's when he looks at me again and just says, "Thank you for making my dream come true." I feel one single tear on my cheek and his face comes near mine so he can kiss it away. Looking up to the stars, not directly looking at him, I say, This is all too much, first of all, you are the most strikingly beautiful man I've ever seen in my life, secondly, you are a prince, third, you married me and forth but not least, you treat me as if I was your most precious possession, you make me feel beautiful, cherished, loved and so sexy. "Because you are all those things and so much more. I will make you forget everyone who at one moment or another hurt you or made you think otherwise and I promise to not let anyone with that intent near you. Will you please believe this is now your life? And most importantly will you please shut up and let me love and get acquainted with the sexy body of my beloved wife?" I pulled him on the bed and wiped that sexy smirk off his precious face with a sensual kiss. This kiss held all my hopes and dreams, but also my fears and questions, he took it all and gave me back, answers, love, strength and trust. He broke the kiss and asked me to open the gift given to me by my children, it's a regular sized box, when I open it, there are three smaller boxes. In the first one I found a ruby heart with a peridot heart incrusted inside, the second had a diamond lightning bolt charm with ruby trimming and the last one was a gold key with an Alexandrite heart in the middle. I could bet I knew what came from whom. He just said, "I had a bit of time with the kids and we came up with these charms, they each have the same one with their birthstone and a heart in the middle with the others birthstone. I thought you'd like that." I just put everything back in the big box and fell into his arms. I got lost in his loving, it was so complete and thorough, and I was being completely pampered for once in my life. Time flew; all of the sudden I felt the warm rays of the arising sun on my back, I laid half on the bed and the rest of me atop him and we just cuddled as I fell asleep in his arms he whispered, "Never forget this night, only a love this strong can endure and surpass all it has. I am here waiting for you forever." don't leave me, not now when I am so happy, please don't! "My Queen, I will find you again, but until then, never forget us, keep your heart open, love is but a whisper away." NO! DON'T GO!

The sun is hot on my face, my head is killing me and I feel the stream of tears on my cheeks. Don't even want to open my eyes, but I know I have to. As soon as I do open them, I just want to cry even more. I was just where it all began, my sofa. I ran into the shower and kept crying (straight out bawling), just sat on the shower floor and let the water fall. I was there for maybe an hour, then I just stood up to really bathe, but then I notice there is something different, the gold chain around my neck with the key charm, also the way my body aches as if I'd been made love to for days, but how can this all be? I don't want to think about this anymore, it was just a stupid dream and the nightmare I call my life began as soon as I awoke. I have to get out of the house, I get out of the shower put on whatever I find first, jump in my car and straight to the beach. I walk in the sand until I can't walk no more, then I almost crawled into the warm, salty water and just let myself be taken away. When my lungs begin to hurt from not getting oxygen, all I could hear in my head and felt in my heart was him, "I'm here. Don't do this to us, please!" I came up for breath and my first real thought was of my children, what the hell was I thinking? Ran out of the water and got in my car all soaking wet and went to pick up my kids. We went home, ate, watched a movie. When they fell asleep, I had myself a glass of wine and just cried over my loneliness. Why dwell on a dream? Live your life at the fullest, take care of what and whom you have right now, because what is destined to be yours, at one time or another will be. We have to have faith that God knows what he's doing. But just to be on the safe side, Babe I'm here waiting for you with the key to unlock our dreams...................

Chastity16

Married

Have you ever thought of hooking up with a married person? A lot of people see it as wrong, I'm not saying that it's right or that there's very serious consequences to deal with or that someone will not be hurt at times, but you never know the circumstances and some things were just meant to be. I myself got involved early on with a married man, with whom I had my first child. After we broke up, I met the man with whom I had my second child and lived with for 4 years and as luck goes, he cheated on me. Then it hit me, "What goes around comes around." But like everybody in similar situations say, "I didn't think I was hurting anybody." You think that because they had some sort of problem at home, it's ok, but usually it's not. Most men lie about their "problems" at home; try to make us feel sorry for them.

I tried not to look at another married man in the way of potential lovers, and succeeded for a very long time, but my will power was done the day I met you. Well literally, we already knew each other, but weren't friends, we reconnected thru the internet of all places and found out how we knew one another; My younger brother and other family members you went to school with, used to play ball with my brother, seeing me in school even though I'm a few years older than you, but was very popular in high school. I'm sorry to say I never ever noticed you in school; truthfully, I didn't think of you as my type of man, still don't. You are shorter than what I usually like, you weren't as popular as you are now and younger, not what I liked or wanted at that moment, but so much of what I need now. Even though you are still short, at this time in my life that is not a real problem anymore, since I've found out that short men have a very nice size package in their pants, Mmmmm. About being younger, that part I really love now, lately my lovers have been younger, even up to 12 years younger.

But back to you; being only 2 years younger, but still have such a cute baby face, you're so handsome and let's not even talk about that beautiful body, (OH MY GOD!!!!). I could touch you all night, running my hands up and down, my lips all over and not even have sex, well sometimes, because you make me so hot I want to jump on you as soon as you walk in the door. I love when you stay the night with me, feeling you there with me, touching me, just feeling you breathe beside me is enough sometimes. We've been together for a little over 1 year and even though I can't say I love you, I do care very deeply for you and if we were to break up or stop seeing each other, I would be very sad and miss you awfully. Sometimes I feel like your girlfriend, that's how special you are, you come to my house at any time of the day and we have sex or just cuddle sometimes, all depending on our mood. You don't care who's at my house to hug and kiss me. I love the way you stay in the house with no shirt as if you were the man of the house, you caress me when I walk by, pinch my butt if you walk by and always kiss me when we meet in the middle. Reading this you'd think I'm in love, but I know better and more than anything, I've learned to protect my heart. I've cried too many tears over men in this lifetime already. You have been my married man fantasy made a reality for over a year, in the whole year we've had 1 real date if you could call it that and it was in a dark movie theater (how sad), but I guess it all comes with seeing or plainly said fucking with a married man. Nothing to expect, no commitments, minimum arguments, no jealousy (yeah right!); this is what we think we want. Even though it has worked till now, I think that with you I want more, you staying over more, going out, having fun together out in the open. I need more sex with you, lots of it, I told you that for us to keep this working you have to come over at least once a week. And the truth is, that's not happening, so I just see other people in between, but still want you back in my bed. I fantasize about riding you on the hammock, you all sweaty, that beautiful tight body beneath me. I want to be able to lick you all over, my lips on everything, but I never know what is too much with you, so our sex has been quite tame, I want more excitement, doing it in a car (not just a finger or two) full blown out sex, going to a motel close to where we live, meeting out in the street for a kiss. You say you don't want this to get emotional, well stop acting like my boyfriend and start being my married lover again. What are you waiting for? If we don't get this back on track this will have to end for good, so pa, let's do this!

Chastity 17

Getting Back

Every woman and even some men have been through heart break. At that exact moment you feel as if you could literally die, as if your life is completely over, you think that person was the most important part of your world. And on the real, it's all bullshit, but at that moment, no one can tell us otherwise. This is mostly toward Latin men, not many want to settle down and less get married, and they only want what's available to them, but once you start talking about it being a relationship, it's over without even really beginning. No ifs, ands or buts to talk about, forget about getting e-mails and less calls, they totally disconnect. I've learned that from the best bullshiters in the world.

Here is something I did or still am doing or maybe just thought up. Who knows? Many women go thru the payback phase; I got stuck there for quite a while. It's where every person of the opposite sex (family has SOME exceptions of course), has to pay for what one bastard or bitch has done to you. I just see it as love them and leave them before they hurt and leave you. This is what usually goes down..................

You meet this person, however the situation, at a party, thru the internet, an old friend or even a friend of a friend. You like what you see and once you get to know them you enjoy the whole package. And if the sex is good, it feels like you just won the lottery. Everything is all good until the monogamous talk comes up, is it just gonna be us? Can I use the B word while talking to my friends about you? What are we to each other? And there it begins. I can play out the let's have sex with other people card very well. After I was hurt many times over by people I thought loved me or at least cared deeply for me. I kind of learned my lesson, as in war, take no prisoners, it's you or them and I decided that it would never be me again; even though I still slip now and then.

When I get hurt again, well anger rolls, tears are cried and we just start all over again.

Lately the people I've met have been thru the internet, the one I'm still seeing at the moment is married. We've been together for more than a year now and if he ever left his wife I would never accept him for myself. Why not? I'd never be able to trust the little cheat, I have been his mistress for over a year and I'm almost sure I'm not the only one. So what do I do? I keep my distance (heart wise), he just doesn't touch me emotionally, don't get me wrong I do have feelings for him, he's a wonderful lover and friend, but that's it, I'm not in love with the guy. The other guy I met, MAN! It was crazy how well we clicked; I couldn't have found anyone more in tune with me even if I was looking. BUT, always a but, for him it was all physical, since he was just getting out of a marriage (or at least that's what he said). It was so natural, as if that person was meant for me, as if he was who I've been waiting for, but I guess my dear God has jokes, because we have such different concepts on what we are and mean to one another. We have sexual dates, I call them that since all we do is have great, hot steaming sex (who am I to complain about that?), but then I look at him while he sleeps and I just start wishing. All the what if's start going thru my mind, what if I could have him all to myself? What if this was real? What if I got pregnant? That's how comfortable we are together or we're just plain stupid, since we not once have used protection. The scary part is when we welcome the thought of having a baby with an almost stranger just because we believe he is the one. I've only felt this way with two people in my whole life, the first one was given the opportunity to hurt me bad when I gave him my heart and the bastard took it, stomped and spit on it, so with this one I'm really trying to not let any of that happen. My strategy to become aloof to these irresistible men, having sex with other gorgeous male specimens. None know of these sexual encounters, but it's not really there problem, is it? Writing these little stories or confessions, however you want to call them, takes up some of my time and relieves some frustration, but nothing like the real thing. The feel of a smooth, hard cock in my hand, my mouth or my waiting, wet pussy is just what the doctor ordered and I can't ever get enough. I am what is called a nymphomaniac, which is kind of a sex addict, I'm insatiable sexually speaking. I love the thought of sex, the feelings, the scent, the intimacy (if only for a few moments). I'll try anything once, twice if I like it and 3 times if it's really good, so men I've had, usually come back at least for the unbelievable sex, which I love to change up constantly. I try to keep them at arm's length, nobody too close to my heart, not even my latest catch, much less him since I really like this guy too much. But we need to learn from our men and not think with our heads, but with our sex, only think of the need you have and fulfilling it with whoever is available at that moment. This is how I live my life, at least for now, at least until one of my fantasy men come and swipe me away.

Chastity18

You Again

Have you ever fallen hard twice for the same person? Well I have, and my opinion is, that its worst the second time around.

I can't believe this, him again and here! I thought I wouldn't have to see him, at least not here. It's been awhile, yes we've crossed paths in the last year, but nothing like being in the same place for 21 days and having to see him almost on a daily basis. I can't tell you how bad I want this asshole, my bad; he just acted as a man that wasn't told the rules. Now he has a live in girlfriend back home, but that's not a big enough reason for me not to want him the same or maybe even more. All the memories come flowing to my mind, taking those long, hot, sexy showers together, that unforgettable night in the pool (you heard about that one) or maybe it's just that easy connection we have once we are close to each other, that's what got me last time and this time I feel I'm going down the same road. The only thing holding me back a bit, is that he is holding back from me, but I'm almost sure he feels as strongly as I do and more so when he tells friends we have in common, that when he sees me he also remembers our times together but mostly the time I was sleeping on his bed and him just looking at how the sun rays reflected off my naked body, saying how I was so special to him. For me that was enough.

The unit had a little get together, where we had some undercover alcohol. Well my ex gets nice and friendly when he drinks, so I'm going try and use that to my advantage. It was a cold night, got to meet and interact with a lot of people I didn't know. In every conversation I was in, he would listen in, but never make any comment even though most of what I said was about him, but only a handful of people knew that. I guess he couldn't take it no more because he texted me to watch where he went and to follow a few moments after. At first I was wary of going, but 5 minutes after he left he texted me again, *We need to talk* I walked as if toward the bathroom and took another way to him. If only he wasn't so damn sexy. I almost bumped into him because it was so dark, but his hands found my waist and he just pulled me to him in a hug, it really felt like coming home. I had to push him away or I would just start bawling and no talking would get done. God, we have this connection, we just click, it's like we were destined to be together. I know he was here because I had made it an issue, we needed to get things clear, I want answers, the way our "relationship" finished was just not doing it for me and that's why we were here now. And stupid me, the first words out of my mouth were I've missed you so fucking much. He just took hold of my hands, his thumbs caressing my palms; even in the darkness I could feel his sadness. But all he said was, "I'm here now, ask all your questions now and whatever is on your mind that you need to tell me also, because I really don't think it's intelligent of me to be alone with you again." Oh damn, I like how that sounds, he still has feelings for me. Ok, why did everything go down as it did? I felt a connection between us from the get go, since the first day I laid eyes on you in Cali. Can you honestly tell me that it wasn't there for you too? Don't you miss the free, liberating way we had sex, anyhow, anytime, anywhere? I do, since I've never felt that free before or after you. "Neither have I" was what he said and while saying this, his left hand sneaks up my neck until he is cradling my cheek, once there he feels the moisture of my tears but says nothing. You need to shut up and stop doing things to me so I can finish before I can't, please. Wasn't I good enough to be your girlfriend? Was I just a notch on your belt? Can you really say you don't miss me in your bed, your pool, your shower? Don't you miss the warmth of my skin by yours in the morning? It was really my wrong, since I never told you how I felt, but you really never felt it? Do you really want to live the rest of your life knowing you made the wrong decisions just because of what other people might think and not by what you feel in your heart? I step up closer, now I'm just a whisper away when I say real close to his lips, do you really want to live without ever again feeling my lips on yours or the way my love clenches when you are deep inside me? At that moment I stand on tip toe and lick his lips. That was all it took to break his resolve, his hands were in my hair, my arms around his waist and the kiss was like always, electrifying. He pinned me against a vehicle and are bodies were completely touching, I could feel his erection against my belly. When his mouth left mine it went to my neck, I had to touch his skin, so my hands went under his shirt and after so long my hands were touching his soft, warm skin. I guess we both just forgot where we were because his mouth found my naked breast, his pants were undone and that erection I came to love was in my hand. Don't ask me how, but I'm sitting on the back of a pickup, he's pulling at my pants, I give in, he whispers in my ear while kissing me "May I have you?" With tears in my eyes, holding him tight against me I respond, I've been yours since I met you, don't have to ask for something that has always been yours, but this has to be the last time, after we get home we go back to how it was, because I want all of you, not only your dick once in a while. He kissed me hard probably to shut me up and slid into me. I felt I wanted to cum right at that moment but didn't want to, wanted to make this last time last forever, but he bit down on my shoulder and I was done. He stayed inside me while my trembling ceased and my tears stopped flowing, but I was crying so hard, I just started making love to him again until he grabbed my face and about to kiss me says, "This will never be over.", cumming inside me. Like I've said before, this man is any woman's dream and at least right now, he is my reality. After a few moments holding each other, we hear our names being called; he still doesn't want to pull out so I move out of his reach. Fixing my clothes, back in control of my emotions I tell him, you never answered any of my questions, the only thing I can say for sure is that our sexual connection is strong, but is there more to it than that for you? Taking me by the arms, he just whispers angrily, "Are you so dense? Don't you see?" No! Tell me!

"Hey we've talking to you, why you ignoring us?" My friends say while laughing at my lost state and blank look, that is at least until they see my tears. My eyes have been focused on him all this time behind the dark sunglasses, dreaming, hoping, wishing, praying, that he tells me let's talk. Maybe my day dream went too far, maybe I will never get to touch his naked skin again or kiss those juicy, delicious lips, but he does owe me that talk, even if what he says hurts, even if just being near him hurts my heart. I look up and he's coming towards me, outstretches his hand and asks, "Can we talk?" Should I? Am I really ready for this? I guess I'll find out since my hand is already in his.

Girls we always fall into their trap or is it our trap? If it didn't work out the first time why should we believe it will the second time around. Maybe because people change or because love moves the world? Keep looking for excuses. Even though not all men are the same, they're quite similar. But you are stronger than anything they throw your way. Just be safe, but always true to yourself. Who knows, maybe it will work, maybe this is who you were destined to be with and just need to each go through these tests. He who doesn't take risks is just not living and I want to live!

Chastity 19

Get Away!

Right now I'm at a moment in life where not much matters. Where so many things have to get done and paid for, when you have almost no time or money for yourself. I'm in dire need of some me time, we all need this mini vacation, at least a few days all to yourself, no family, kids, pets, housework, nothing, just me, myself and I, as the song says. So I just say "Fuck it", take what's left in my credit card and book me a weekend in Jamaica, got a cheap flight and little hotel for 3 nights. I need to get away. I tell almost everyone that I'm going on a military trip and will not have much access to a phone, let 2 or 3 people in on what I'm really doing and going, you never know.

I arrive at Sangster International Airport in Montego Bay and a shuttle from the hotel is there to pick me up. Already feeling better, the atmosphere is so relaxing; the music just takes you away. Almost fell asleep on the short ride to the Idle Away Resort, which is a cute little thing. My bags are taken to my room while I check in, a local drink is given to me by the front desk clerk as a welcome cocktail (right now can't even remember the name of it). I love the accent, even that has a relaxing loll to it. I'm beat, so I go straight to my room and only ask for a bowl of fruit. The hotel is nice and inexpensive, but let me tell you, the room is beautiful, a lot of explosive colors and lots of exotic flowers. I sit on my balcony drinking wine and eating fruit, while looking out to the beach and listening to the music from the lobby downstairs. After about 30 minutes I see a couple strolling hand in hand down the beach, looks so romantic, there's something I've never done. I'm the freakiest woman in the world and I've never had a moonlit beach stroll, so I decide, what the fuck I'll go by myself and enjoy a bit of this beautiful night. I put on a 2 piece leopard print bikini with a brown sarong, going barefoot.

Leave my key at the front desk so I don't have to carry anything and let him know where I'm at (just in case). The air is a bit balmy and humid, but it's so perfect, the white sand still feels warm beneath my feet, even the water is a comfortable temperature if I wanted to jump in. I walk for about an hour, till I reach the rocky part of the beach, where I sit on the sand and just breathe deeply. A few moments later I notice someone sitting on a rock high above me, just looking out to the sea, all I see is the profile of his body, looks firm, hard, strong, his face, the left side of it at least, since it's what I can see, I have to say it has a uniqueness to it, he looks exotic like the land I am in, but at the same time he looks so alone, so empty, his eyes just staring into the darkness as if he could see the waves coming in, which I know he can't, but he keeps looking not even noticing me and I've been there for about 15 minutes. It's time for me to get back because if I don't, I'll climb up those rocks and sit next to him and caress his cheek, just so he doesn't feel as alone as I do, maybe then we could just conquer our loneliness together, so rather than doing something I might regret in the morning I walk slowly and thoughtfully to my room. Too tired to think much once I'm there, so took a quick warn shower and crashed in bed.

Woke up to a magnificent morning, sun shining thru my patio door and I'm feeling relaxed and energized. I called room service to bring me my breakfast and was reminded of my little tour trip to Negril Cliffs for cliff jumping (for me probably just watching it) and then to the Pirates Cove to have some fun on the party boats. Was already dressed for it since all I brought for the trip were bathing suits, t-shirts and shorts, so I had a nice calm breakfast on my patio, just looking out to the beach, when the picture of that man popped in my head sending shivers thru me, maybe I should've gone to him last night, then I wouldn't have so many questions about him today. No time for regrets and what ifs right now, going to have me some fun while in my much fantasized about vacation in Jamaica. The cliffs were like unbelievable, couldn't even look down without feeling dizzy and I'm not really scared of heights; most tourists didn't dare jumped and just watched the inlanders do their thing, but there was a daredevil from down under, Australia, he jumped in a few times in many different ways. I was in awe in him, handsome fellow, his name is Jack. I was just being a watcher, until Jack dared me into jumping, I screamed all the way down, it's been one of the most exhilarating things I've ever done in my entire life, thought I was going to have a heart attack, but when I broke to the surface, I felt alive, like

I could do anything. As soon as I get to the top, I thanked Jack with a big kiss in front of everyone and went to my bus to go to Pirates Cove and have fun in the very much talked about party boats. It really wasn't very far from where we were diving, real nice marina, once there well it looks like fun but prices were a little too steep for me, so I had a drink in 1 of the shacks there and found out about the caves in Pirates Cove. Was told that if I didn't want to jump off the cliffs (once is enough), I could go down some types of steps all the way down to the caves and swim there. It was already about 3:30, so I thought I'd have at least a good 2 hours to be there, so there I went. I wish I'd bought a water proof camera, because this is mesmerizing. Was kind of scared since I was by myself, but not enough to make me leave. Swam to the rocks and ventured further into the caves, it was a stunning sight, the way the sun glared off the minerals and rocks, all the different colors. Don't know how long I've been there for, but as soon as I felt the water at my feet, kind of knew I was in a bit of trouble. Ran out of the cave and dove head first into the water, but now I couldn't find the way I had gotten there and the current was pulling me hard God knows where. Now I'm panicking (nice, gonna die on my vacation), looking for a way out, trying to stay calm so I could think clearly. I think I can hear someone yelling, but can't make out what they're saying, so I just start yelling back. All the sudden I feel something grab my hips, now I'm really screaming, start kicking wildly, that's until his head comes out of the water and says, "Oww that hurt love." I was so happy to see him (whoever he is), I'm not alone anymore, and I'm getting out of here. The excitement went to my head and I kissed him hard, his hands were still on my hips so he pulled me closer and deepened the kiss (talented kisser this guy). His hand slides down to my crotch thru the front of my bikini, he freezes there, I think remembering we don't know each other, but I'm too into this to stop now, so I caress his lips with my tongue, suck on his juicy lower lip and bring my hand down to his, urging him to continue where he stopped. My hands roamed his hard, dark body, while our kiss never ended, his hand making my love sing just for him. He could feel me about to erupt like a volcano, so he lifted me and instructed me to wrap my legs around his waist while he walked to a stone wall with his back against the wall, he shoved my bikini bottom to the side then just held my pussy in his hand, whispering in my ear "So hot" I just moaned into his neck. He grabbed my legs so I would let go of his waist and laid me back as if to float, really didn't know what he was doing, but really didn't care. While floating with my feet on his chest, he opened my legs and put them on each of his shoulders, his hands are once again on my hips (now I know where this is going). His mouth hot on my swollen clit, his tongue now in me, such a nice, thick tongue to have in my pussy and this man knows how to fuck me good like this, just when I think I can't take it much longer he stops fucking me with his tongue and starts licking my whole pussy in long, slow strokes, sucking on my clit and biting gently on my lips on his way up and down. Now I'm really going to drown, but he saves me again, he pulls me to his body, sliding my pussy down his broad chest, flat stomach and right on to what feels to be a very big, rock hard cock. He has to be at least 8-9 inches and very thick, since I can feel every movement, every inch of that enormous dick, I cum so fast and hard it's not even funny, I bit his shoulder and neck hard; but this is not over, he kisses me with so much passion while sliding out of my still wanting pussy, he turns me toward the wall and gives it to me from behind. He is so big it hurts, but it's a good hurt, my kitty loves the pressure of being this stretched out, I feel it all more. His hands find my breasts (which me being a 42DD isn't very hard), while nibbling on my ear and neck he pinches my nipples with each inward thrust. Simultaneously we cum, him holding me tightly to his chest, if not, I would've floated away, I turn around and just look at him, so dark and handsome, but what pulls me in is his eyes, caramel colored and so sexy. I just have to kiss him again, after a few minutes and almost losing control again he tears himself away from me and says, "My name is Dante and I think we really need to get out of here, like now." I had even forgotten where we were for a moment there, but he woke me up fast. He said we'd need to swim under a stone wall, a quick swim is what he says; I'm not a bad swimmer, but I don't even snorkel, so now I'm nervous. He explained exactly where and how we would do it so I could go first, making sure I got thru. The swim was about 15-20 seconds, but felt a lot longer, he came up right beside me not 5 seconds after I had surfaced, we swam together to the steps I used to come down. Again he let me go first, but was close behind me. I walked to my bus, once there he tells me to get my things because I'll be riding back with him on his motorcycle. I only had a small bag and he did save me, how was I to say no? Before leaving the cove we had an early dinner on me (he fought over that), and talked a bit, turns out me hero Dante is also my lonely stranger from the beach. What a wonderful coincidence! It was a very nice ride back; he was taking it slow so he could tell me about the different places we were passing by, best tour of the day. Once we make it back to the hotel, he asks me to take a stroll with him on the beach as soon as we are done taking a shower and changing. Again? How can I say no? He goes God knows where, while I take a hot, bubble bath in the Jacuzzi. My muscles are hurting from all the swimming, the jets and the heat of the water is so soothing. I start massaging my legs with the loofah sponge and afterwards just let myself go, fell asleep while thinking of my dark rescuer. I was surprised awake by the jets spraying me again, but the biggest surprise of all was finding myself looking into captivating caramel eyes. I jumped up; almost fell when I slip in the tub, but as lately, he rescued me from that fall also. What are you doing in here? Is all I can think of saying while standing naked in his arms, he looks down at me and says, "I got restless waiting for you in the lobby, called the room and no answer, so I told my buddy Andy from the front desk to get me a key since you seem to be quite accident prone and that we were kind of seeing each other." Incredible, I would get fired for doing something like that, but he asked for me to please not be mad at his friend. How could I be? Time to get untangled from him and put some clothes on (not that I really want to), so we can go for our walk. A real romantic, moonlit stroll on the beach, with a strikingly gorgeous man, who can ask for more? Well not me, but thank God, I got more. It was so romantic, we walked hand in hand down the beach, stopping for seashells and kisses, we went to the place I first saw him, we sat on the sand and talked about the feeling of loneliness we were both going thru and how sometimes even a little bit of affection is better than none at all. I stood and danced to my own tune in knee high water, my white, gauze dress getting all wet. He's just looking at me smiling (probably thinks I'm crazy), I pull him up; he grabs me in a bear hug and twirls me around. We fall laughing on the wet sand, kissing, touching, I get serious while caressing his cheek and just blurt out, you are so beautiful. He stares at me and tells me no one has ever used that word as an adjective towards him, I just say, good I'm your first. Now he gets up pulling me with him and slowly walks backwards into the water (I'm holding back, sharks!), but he cheats, starts kissing me while walking and I go like a moth to a flame. We walk till I am chest deep and then the touching begins all over. At last I feel that big, thick monster, even beneath the water it feels hot and it's so hard. I can feel my kitty start to throb, pulsate, asking for what she had a taste of, but still needs much more. His fingers find my expectant pussy and play with her till my hips start thrusting into his hand, then he takes me fast and hard, we were done in mere minutes, at any other occasion I'd say 3 minutes don't work, but these were the most satisfying minutes I've had in a long time. We stay hugging for a bit and walk out of the water side by side, my arm around his waist and his big, black hand on my creamy, white hip holding me tight to him all the way back to the room. There we shower together, lathering each other up but just kissing, once out of the shower I put a towel around my breasts, he swoops me up in his arms and carries me to the bed, where we kiss some more and get to know one another intimately. I found the spot on his body that with just a whisper of a caress makes him shiver, while he found one on mine that makes my eyes roll back. It was a unique experience, having someone, almost a stranger at that, explore your body so boldly and completely, the whole moment just felt right. We fall asleep while he was still hard in me, glorious way to wake up.

Woke up to those soulful eyes looking at me, taking me in. I just smile and stretch a bit, my body was aching, but in a good way. He kissed me and told me to get ready to see more of Jamaica; he'd be waiting at the front of the hotel on his bike in 1 hour. Right at that moment my tummy decided to growl, he kissed it and told me our first stop would be a home cooked breakfast, not a problem with that, I'll be down in 1 hour. What a sight! Him on his bike in shorts, a t-shirt and really dark sunglasses. It was a short ride, about 15 minutes, he stops in front of a cute little place, we walk in as if it were his house, in the living room we are greeted by an older woman with a huge smile, which became bigger and brighter once Dante kissed her cheek (seems to have that effect on women), it was something special to watch. She asked me what I'd like for breakfast while seating us at a beautiful, old, cherry oak, 12 person table, I was kind of lost because everything seemed cozy or homey, not like a bed & breakfast or little shop, but I answered, eggs, toast and coffee please. She turned to Dante and says, "I know what you'll have." He looks at me while smiling and tells me that's his grandmother, I am so ashamed, I get up and go straight into the kitchen, just to be showed out by her while telling me, "Any friend of my grandbaby is welcome for breakfast in our home, and even more one that has brought my baby's smile back. I owe you for that, it seems."At that she winks at me and blows him a kiss. I wanted to leave so bad, while Dante just laughed at me. Have to say breakfast was delicious, but I argued till I won about doing the dishes, which I made

Dante help, least I could do. After showing me around and extending an invitation back, she left to the grocery store, leaving us to our own. He, like I, was brought up by his grandmother, so I can understand the love there. It is so cool to have ones personal tour guide to show you the best not known places, not only the hot tourist spots and have him kiss you all at the same time. Our last stop was at Whoopie's, where the view was hypnotizing, the white sand, low orange sun on the bluest water imaginable. That was what Dante had as a background; he had taken his shirt off, all those muscles, God! And to think I have to go home tomorrow. We walked the beach in silence for a little while and decided that we'd head back to the hotel for dinner as soon as the sun set. He jumps on the bike and pulls me to him and we just start making out, he sits me in front but facing him all this without breaking the soul searing kiss, just the way I've seen it so many times while fantasizing, my legs on top of his thighs, our bodies are as close as they can get. I didn't even notice him turning on the bike until it was vibrating under me, the sensation of him and the motorcycle was mind blowing, but he always kept my orgasm 1 step away. He opened his pants and took out that big, delicious, chocolate dick while with the other hand he was pulling my shorts and panties to the side to make way for him. I was gone, laying back on the handle bars taking it all in; the beautiful sky, the feel of Dante deep inside of me and the way my body trembled from the vibrations of the motorcycle. We came together soooo hard, soooo long, just as the sun was setting, soooo perfect. We got cleaned up and headed back to the hotel, had a lite supper and went to my room to chill in the Jacuzzi a bit. It was bittersweet, but nice. We talked about our past, present and what we wanted and dreamed of for the future. After the bath, we sat on the balcony on a lounge chair, just cuddling, kissing and talking some more, we sat there till the sun came up.

My last morning in Jamaica, my plane leaves in 8 hours, we've only slept for about 2, but I can always sleep on the plane. We lay here entangled, his hard dick pressed against my ass, his hand caressing and pinching my breast while he bites my back and shoulder. How much longer can I make believe I'm still asleep? Not much longer I find out. The sensation of him biting my back was too much, it's something I've always done but was never done to me, and it feels incredible! Almost came with just that but he doesn't play that, he has more in mind for me. He turns me completely on my belly and whispers, "You can make believe you're asleep all you want ma, I'm still getting mine." With that said he starts at the nape of my head, biting, kissing and all the while slowly descending, shoulder blades, love handles, butt, hips, my thighs (there I got plenty excited but he kept going down), to that sensitive spot behind ones knees, calves, heel, then he bit the arch of my sole and started sucking one by one each of my toes. Why didn't I come to Jamaica sooner? Opens my legs wide, tilts my pelvis up, and brings his face so close I can feel his breath on my pussy. I slowly start sliding towards him, but he just pushes me away while saying, "Patience, my love." Whoever knows me knows that that is not possible. One virtue God did not bestow plentiful enough of on me or maybe it's just that I don't know how to use it to my advantage, is patience. I just pout, making believe I am mad, he just couldn't resist it and starts laughing. With that beautiful smile still in place, he takes one lick, it was a languid, long, slow lick, every hair on my body stood to attention; I wasn't mad anymore and he wasn't laughing either. He ate me as if I was to be his last meal, calmly, leisurely, enjoying every lick and nibble. I came so many times I lost count, every time better and harder than the last; I was amazed at how easily and fast I was wet for him again and again. Then I don't know if he was taking a little break or just giving me one, at least that's what I thought, until I felt his hard rod deep inside, I was expecting a licking and instead got a sticking. He got in so deep in the position I was in, I thought it'd come out my throat, but you're not gonna hear me complaining none, maybe moaning, but never complaining. It was fast and hard (well if you consider 20 minutes fast), I came again, but then I wanted to make it all for Dante. I got to moving my ass and clenching that magnificent cock with my hot, wet pussy until I milked him completely. He just collapsed on the bed, gasping for air, but all the same with a big, silly grin on his beautiful mouth. He grabbed me in a bear hug, almost couldn't breathe and then softly whispered in my ear, "Never have quite been so content with a woman before." I didn't say a single word, I just sighed since I know this was just what it was. We took a quick shower together and back to bed, but only gentle caresses and touches were exchanged, it was like memorizing each other, every little nook and cranny. He fell asleep and I just looked at him, what a beautiful man and like always the what if's came to mind, but I just pushed them away. Waited till he was out like a light to get off of the bed, my things were packed so I called the front desk to send someone up to take them down, I dressed quietly and kissed him gently on the lips. Left a note on my pillow saying,

"Thank you for most importantly saving my life and for being my personal tour guide. I will always have beautiful and fond memories of my Jamaican paradise. Please tell your grandmother that if I ever come back, I will definitely look her up, kisses to her. Here I leave you my email: sxychastity@yahoo.com that's if you ever want to contact me after leaving you this cowardly way, but I couldn't say goodbye while looking into those soulful eyes. And thank you also for making my fantasy trip a tremendous reality, only with you. Please make your dreams come true that is what I want most for you; let me believe I was part of it all. You will always have a piece of my heart in Jamaica.

Love,
Your Sxy Portorican

I got everything in order at the hotel and let them know my companion was to be leaving later and not to be disturbed. The trip home was uneventful, but who am I to lie? I already miss my Jamaican.

We should all take a vacation or two and just go wild; no one can judge you, only God. Let the men look at you with lust and the women with envy, don't be embarrassed of your body, you have to love yourself before anybody else loves you. My advice, take your first trip by yourself, even if it's not out of the country but far enough from where you live, so no one knows you, and there, get away.

Chastity 20

Same Sex

This is a bit different than the other stories I've written, but doesn't mean it's not sexy. Ever had a person of your same sex crush on you? As in flirting with you, telling other friends they would love to taste you and touch your skin just to see if it's as soft as it looks? Or have you ever looked at a person of your same sex and had the urge to kiss them or just lick their whole body? I think we all go thru this, we just don't know how to talk about it or even who to talk about it that won't look at as weird. But let's talk about it now.

I've been on this internet site for a while now, called Adult Friends Fucking, been e-mailed by a lot of different and strange people, even couples in which the point of contact is always the male, from a lot of different places. But one e-mail was different, the site nick was coconut kisses, it was from a woman. I decided to e-mail her back so I didn't seem rude but off the bat I did let her know I love me some dick and wasn't interested in becoming a pussy eater, she laughed at that and we became fast friends. She took our friendship and ran with it; after a few e-mails she asked for my number which I gave, we talked on the phone lots of times and let me tell you she sounds like the coolest person, divorced, has grown children, hard worker and a very good listener. I've learned in our talks that she's bisexual, either or she's going to have it. We talk about our past experiences, people we are sexing at the moment and as they say, curiosity killed the cat and I had to ask about how it is being with another woman. She answers all my questions as a teacher would, calm and simple, as time went by my questions started getting a bit more intimate and she started asking more often when we could finally meet, I held that meeting off for as long as I could, but truth of the matter I did want to meet her, she had become my friend in the months we had e-mailed, texted and talked and she was offering me a once in a lifetime deal, for my curiosity to be fulfilled to whatever point I wanted it to, she would answer ALL my questions and do me till I said stop, no hard feeling or strings attached.

First time we met we just checked each other out, she wasn't the most beautiful woman but she is very attractive and she is so cool it really didn't matter. She French kissed me off the bat and kept talking as girlfriends would, so my nervousness went out the window. I wasn't home alone that first time, but by the time she was about to leave we both wanted a bit more, so she asked me to take a ride with her, we went to a nearby beach which at that time of night was pitch black (Good so no one would see me and if they did probably wouldn't recognize me). We kissed some more, she's touching me all over, my hands go to her enormous tits, take one out and pop it in my mouth, I start sucking on it like I like a man to suck on mine, all the while she's too busy finger fucking me, tasting me off her own fingers but after awhile she tires of doing it that way so she puts my seat back, opens my legs, moves my panties and shorts to the side and dives in. that girl can eat a pussy with the best of men or even better (getting wet just thinking of it). We kissed more there, since we couldn't once we got back to my place and planned our first real date.

Ok, ladies and gentleman, now this was a date. Not one single man has treated me with such gentleness and romanticism ever, she took me on a full date, dinner, drinks and really talked, for awhile it was like 2 girls out and about just chillin', but I knew what was next and believe me, I was really yearning for it. Crazy when you think about it, I say I'm 100% straight but here I am yearning for a person of my same sex to kiss and touch me. Once we made it to the motel I was a bit ashamed and even turned away when the guy came up to the car, she did everything like a guy would. While it's just her and myself I'm ok, but other people just make it too real. Once in the room I kinda got shy but she just flowed with it, she gave me space got me some wine to loosen up, massaged my shoulders while kissing my neck, turned me around and then we really started making out (which by the way is always great). The touching begins and the clothes start coming off without ever breaking the kiss (men take notes), her mouth goes down my neck, to my shoulder and finally my breast. She starts nibbling on it, suck, bite, lick one then the other, while her hand finds my oh so wet pussy, as soon as she begins fucking me with her fingers I cum;

she calls me a bad girl because I had to wait for her tongue to be there. So we start kissing again and she kinda turns sideways and opens my legs putting one on either side of her as hers on me, our pussy lips are touching (this is one thing I have always been curios about how it would feel), it feels sooo good, we start grinding into each other; so wet and tender, I was about to cum again, she knew this, stopped, pushed me away but only to grab my hips and bury her face into my craving pussy, she ate me like no man till this day has. The girl really wanted that cum, she stayed there till my orgasm was done and another on its way, but she let that one come with our pussies playing together. We were both done after that one, just chilled on the bed, her hands always on my body; see women love to cuddle after sex, so it was perfect. After a while we showered together which was quite fun, she made what I thought would be an awkward first time into a fun and romantic experience. We dressed while stealing looks, kisses and tender touches. The ride home was just 2 girlfriends coming back from a fun night in the town, talking about men, our likes and dislikes and of course she asked if there would be a next time for us. A question I really couldn't answer at that exact moment, but I did say I really wanted us to remain friends, at that she smiled, guess she understood. Who knows? I have many male friends, 1 girlfriend couldn't hurt............. Jajajajaaja. Curiosity killed the cat, but my kitty purred at being so masterfully licked. Always thought I should try everything at least once, like it? Do it as many times as you like. Take a risk, what is there to lose? Except the experience.

Chastity 21

The Beach

Where were we this time? Weapons qualification in "beautiful, hot" Salinas. First day was a drag since everyone was tired, so we settled with just having a few beers right outside our room and talking about guys we've had and the ones we had our eyes on. It was to be an early night since the next day was to be a very long one, but plans for Saturday night were already being made.

What a day Saturday has turned out to be, up at 0500 hours and our day went till almost 2200 hours, but I still wanted to go out for at least a lil' while. The stress of the work week and wanting to finish with the whole zero, qualification and classes today had me feenin' a drink fiercely and my girl Lyn never lets me down. She had been invited out by some guys from another unit for some drinks and billiard, so that's where went. When we got there I see it's just a Cash & Carry around the way, cute lil' place, ok music, not a lot of booze to choose from, 1 single pool table and an outdoor sitting area. Lyn's friends are so cool, the only problem is that there's 5 of them and only 2 of us, which at first was not a problem since we were just chillin'. But to be truthful (as I always am), I had my eye on a particular one of them since we got there and when introductions were done that I finally heard his voice it was on. Being as close in tastes as we are, Lyn liked him too, thank God he has a lil brother that was feelin' Lyn like crazy, at that, we were set to begin the games.

G and I kinda fell into a conversation all by ourselves, the rest of the group would try to jump in and we would unintentionally push them out, and it was like that most of the time we were at the bar. We played pool against one of the other guys and won, I cheated a bit but not a lot, since I was grinding and putting my tits on the guy, but just so he couldn't concentrate on the game, while I'm doing this to him my eyes are on G, he was definitely getting a rise outta that; knowing that I want him but flirting with another. But like I said, we won. We stayed there till the employees started putting chairs up and turning off lights, that was like at 0215, I guess they didn't know how to tell us to leave, jajaja, we asked if we could buy some beer to go, of course they said yes, we bought about 2 dozen and headed out. Where to go? Everywhere is closed, so we went to the beach and drank some more. The guys started taking off their shirts, now that was quite a view, at least 3 of them were worth looking at, the other 2 tried without avail. The guys we intended to fuck looked delicious, 1 looked firm and trim a body of a boxer, while the other was muscular and hard as a weight lifter. My girl Lyn had the fit guy while I couldn't wait to touch the hard muscles; they were just in their underwear in less the 15 minutes, who can blame them with those bodies. My, my, my, I couldn't stop staring at either of them, even though we already knew which one was to be with whom. Once we got down to our undies we hit the water, crazy as it sounds, it was about 0330 but the water felt great. The guys started getting the idea that we girls already knew who we wanted, so the fuckers left, but the bastards left 3 behind instead of just 2, probably just to fuck with us. Lyn and I, we didn't care, we got our respective guys and started to play. Mmmmm that first kiss was just luscious, he was so attentive to my needs, everything was simple, effortless, if we had planned it, it wouldn't have been so perfect. Not even because we were by the main road stopped us, we weren't even concerned about the people seeing us fuck out in the open, we even forgot about the other guy. My concentration was all on G from that first kiss, first touch; he seized my full attention.

The way he touched my body was sexy, I was putty in his masterful hands. I felt like a submissive tending to her master, his will was my command, whatever he wanted I gave without question and what he desired he took without asking. And the way he kissed me left me gasping, not for air but for more of his kisses, for his body on mine, for him deep inside of me. This didn't take long; right there on the hood of the car he put my panty to the side and thrust hard and deep into my hot, wet cunt, it felt so damn good. We kept kissing which only made me hornier and since I already like so much what he is dishing out, why stop? I can't even put into words the feelings of desire that were coursing thru my body, the man knew what he was doing to me and he was doing it oh so right. He wants to dominate my body in the worst way; he wants to be the Master to this Mistress, at least sexually speaking. Now I take the reins for a bit as I do as I want or so I think; making him withdraw from my pussy just so I can give my back to him, wanting to feel him completely, his length, his girth, all that beautiful cock in me. Then I really started pumping his dick, we were meeting thrust for thrust, I wanted his milk so bad, but he said "not yet", took his cock out of my throbbing pussy (thought I was gonna start crying) and started massaging my butt cheeks with that magnificent dick, slowly just putting the head in my kitty and taking it out when I tried to grind against him, smothering my asshole with his precum, till I was almost asking for it (and I'm not too into anal), but as soon as he felt it ready he took what he said belonged to him. It was hurting a bit (no lube), but as soon as he bit my back while his hand was busy with my clit and fingering my pussy, nothing else mattered. First man to make me wanna give up the ass, not emotionally but sexually. Girls you know there's a point in the relationship where you give anything and everything to that one special guy, but wouldn't if you didn't think it'd last, well we're talking about swallowing the cum and the ass. This guy got the ass sexually, almost making me beg for him to hurry up and put it in and I've not encountered many men that could do that. Let's get back to the damn story.....

After about 30-45 minutes of crazy, mind blowing sex, we take a breather. Lyn was already on her way towards us with baby brother. She said it was time to move, since it was already close to 0500 and our first formation was 0600 (where did time go?). I couldn't believe so much time had gone by and the reality of it all was I wasn't done with him yet. I want to dominate this man who is almost a stranger but still has this infinite control over my body. There was a promise of more private moments to come. I'm just hoping they're REALLY, REALLY SOON!!!!

Chastity 22

The End

The tears were rolling down my face before you even uttered the words, I knew tonight was when you finally got the nerves to end our 2 year affair. How? Well you're behavior gave you away, I saw you less than I've ever had before, in bed you were distant, you wouldn't even kiss me anymore. But never would I have thought that it would hurt this fucking much. I kind of imagined us ending up together, just you and I. What an idiot I was! Having you here saying that you had someone else and that she was important enough for you to leave your wife and just come and dump me after all this time was like a smack in the face. And to think I love you, me loving you, you lil smurf of a man. In part I also had fault in this, I let myself go with you, my rules were kicked to the curve as soon as I met you, what kind of rules you may be asking? Well to start, the staying over and sleeping together, then we got you meeting my friends and of course the most important, you meeting my children. Before I used to say that if you ever left her I'd never be in a serious relationship with you, I guess I was just using that as a defense mechanism, because now I know I would've taken you and just loved you more than I do now. You were the closest thing to a boyfriend I ever had, I ever wanted, but this is what happens when you open up and let them in, they hurt you and those close to you. The worst of it all was when you said you had no type of loving feelings toward me , for you it was just a sexual affair, 2 years together and you felt nothing for me, such a cold hearted bastard.

How dare you ask me to still, after all this, be friends? Have you no shame? After all we shared, you really think I would just want to talk to you? Maybe hang out? NEVER! You are still too important to me for that. I don't even have the faintest idea of how I'll react when I do see you with her; one thing's for sure, it'll hurt like hell. Just so you know, when I do get over you and these stupid ass feelings, I'll be a stronger woman and more of a bitch than before, you are the type of man that make women like me harder and more difficult for the good men that DO still exist out there; I just hope that the special man that God has put on this Earth for me can see thru this veil of deceit that I opted to put up to the world, has the patience to wait me out and break down this stupid wall that will be between us and mostly help me believe a good man can and does think that I am a truly special and beautiful woman in my own right, because you have just made me feel cheap, dirty and ugly, but that too will pass because I know in my heart that God doesn't make mistakes, just maybe 1, and that was you, (☺), but for you I will be thankful to him also. Because from this I will learn and get up again, because now I know I'm capable of loving again, I just have to be wary of whom I let into my soul next time. Most of my stories are real, all from the heart, but as you know me and my writing not all have a happy ending, because our stories don't end till we die. To you JV, have a great life. To me, a great new beginning.

Chastity23

Best Female Friend (BFF)

You guys know that all I need is an idea or stray thought to get the ball rolling. This is really different, but I AM an all around type of gal. This one is about female friendships, when we think we have them at least. Why write about this? Well mostly women will be reading my book so they need to open their mind to what our BFF is feeling or maybe they might be feeling I don't know how to put into words and to the guys that read it, this is a much clearer look into our heads and the most important reason is that if I don't get this out of my sexy lil mind no naughty thoughts are filtering in. ;-)

Friendship is defined as: the relationship of trust, faith and concern for each other's feelings. It's a relationship of mutual caring and intimacy among one another. A friend is one who knows you as a person and regards you for what you are and not what he or she is looking in a good friend. Also is a feeling of comfort and emotional safety with a person. It's when you don't have to weigh your thoughts or measure your words; it's when someone knows you better than yourself.

At least that's what I found when I googgled it. Some so true, but the word has a very big range for people to give their opinions on it. I do believe that if you regard me as a friend then you have to be there 200% just as I will be; I give you all my trust from the get go, so I'll believe anything you tell me, good or bad, if I catch you in a lie or talking about things we've discussed in private, you will have just 1 more chance and my trust will not be the same. I try never to expect ANYTHING out of ANY type of relationship, be it friends or lovers. Why? Because I always get disappointed when I do. I can be your best, truest, most loyal friend as I can also be the baddest, bitch of an enemy you ever encounter, but let's not go there. I'm just gonna let you in on how I am as a friend:

loyal till the first lie, giving till I feel taken advantage of, loving till I see I'm the only one that cares, trustworthy, I will always be there to listen to you, be it good or bad and even if we fall out and never speak to each other, our conversations will always be confidential. But I am a real friend, so be prepared to hear stuff you probably don't want to hear, I'll give you advice without you asking for it and I'll be in your grill 'bout shit that isn't my problem, but as a friend ANYTHING that I think will harm you , is already hurting you or yours is my problem. If you leave my out of the loop, I'll think as I am now, that you don't trust me or I'm just not enough of a friend to you.

One thing that I think each woman out there should know is that between us girls there's a code, somewhat different at times, cause of circumstances or closeness with the female. Just like males we call dibs on guys, but unlike them, once a friend has put her eye on that certain man, the others will not touch that. We also self sacrifice for our girls, as in chillin' with a hot guys friend so our girl can get some alone time with Mr. Hot Guy. But what should be the #1 Golden Rule is that our girls come before any guy. Why? Because we are like family and men come and go, while we are there for you forever. Men are a dime a piece, we, good, best friends are Priceless.

Think about it. And remember a BFF is a hard thing to find but a very easy thing to lose.

Chastity 24

Empty

Questions with no answers, feelings hurt, hearts broken (or maybe just egos crushed). When one, all and maybe other of these things happen we usually feel incomplete, unsatisfied and in some instances so empty, an ugly kind of emptiness happens mostly when we use it referring to sexual relationships. That I can remember I've felt it twice, felt used and abused as if the person sucked the soul outta my body and just trampled it; you don't need to be in love or even in a serious relationship, maybe just think that this person will be around for a while. Let me tell you what happened to me and make it clearer.

I met this guy thru friends, I'd seen him before but no click at the moment, but when we were put together on a blind date (not so blind since we'd seen each other just not interacted), it was a very nice evening and I saw what I've been missing out on, so I thought to myself, "Maybe this is someone I should get to know better." OK guys!!! We did have sex that first night, but we are adults and why wait if we both want it; at first it was outta control, as if he couldn't get enough of me, then we caught our breath and things got even better. He can definitely kiss, so I was hooked. I wanted a second try at him ASAP, so the next night we all got together again. That turned out to be a fucking big mistake. He sounded excited at getting together again but as soon as we were together he was cold towards me, not a kiss not even a hug until I mentioned it, then he was the guy I went out with the night before, even more touchy-feely. Got to a nice, dark location, had a few drinks, goofed around with the other couple for a bit till they left to do their thing, he took my hand and we walked until we found a nice spot to spend some alone time, took us a while to figure out how to do what we wanted to (FUCK), but eventually we got it or not. Guess he wasn't feeling me, the position or maybe just the whole place, when he just stopped and said, "It's kinda fucked up, twice and both times uncomfortable." My problem was mostly the way he said it, as if I was doing it on purpose, when the reality of it all was that I really wanted to get to know him better, be with him, feel close to him. Then he just said he was gonna get his things and leave since we were close enough to where he was staying he could walk there, that was THE slap in the face. He interrupted the other couple to get his shit and without any more explanations he gave me a kiss on the cheek and left. I was so embarrassed, everything seemed as if it had been me, something I did or (involving a male in the mix) something I didn't, but wasn't even that, I was so willing to be with him. At that moment and still now I felt stupid, dirty, like nothing, a piece of trash. How can a grown man go so low as to treat a woman like that? But when we women are single and feeling lonely we feel more than we should, sometimes doesn't even have to be about him, it's about us, what we want and mostly what we need. I have my own things, house, car, material stuff; those are things I wanted, some I needed for myself or my family. When I think about a man in my life, it's because I want him there, not because I need him and at this point of my life (God only knows why) I want him, really want him, maybe cause it seems he has multiple personalities, the sweet one, the one that cuddles, kisses, caresses me, then there's the sexually aggressive guy, the one that seems as if he couldn't get enough of me, this guy is passionate, rough and so damn sexy, the way he pins me down while kissing, I love the way he takes charge about everything sexual, with those two personalities I have NO problem, it's the third gut that fucks us over; he's angry, impatient, he has no concern for my feelings, he has a way to make me feel no type of connection with him, which at the same time gets me sincerely angry, even more when I know there's something there and it would be a great ride for both of us, if we could just control his bipolar tendencies. I would love to hear from anyone who's had a guy like this one, just so I could find out how to cope (because I want to). But for now, I just hope he apologizes and we can give it another try, just 1 more, that's it! I'm not that starved for male attention and I do have more admirers, but at this moment they're just not him. ;-)

Chastity 25

Some Sexy Training

Gotta love the Army!!! So many men so little time............. My unit is getting ready to deploy and we are training every which way across the US of A; too much fun to be serious for long. Where we're at now is too cold for comfort, don't even wanna think about getting naked, that is unless tall, dark and gorgeous asks me to. Oh and did he!!!

This is the best training I've taken in the many years I've been in the service, we are treated as adults that we are, we go and do what is needed and come back to rest for the next day. The instructors are the same for many trainings, I think they went and got the baddest, buffest, most knowledgeable, best looking instructors in the whole Army (not all of them mind me, but most). While many caught my eye, I'll have to say the half Portorican, half Dominican had me all, nice brown skin, hair and sexy bedroom eyes, about 6'2", very nicely built, other than that, the mother fucker was fine and sexy to boot. I played it off for a cool minute, since this is a training environment, but 4 days was enough of seeing him and not saying anything personal, so as always I brought it home. Other than write I can take some mean pictures, so during training I made sure he was in many of them, plus in videos. At the end of the day I asked him if he had a problem with me posting them on the internet, he said none at all, then I offered my business card so he could get in touch with me thru e-mail and see them and he accepted with a smile. You see my card other than my e-mail has my cell phone number and he understood the reason of me giving him that card, guess he wanted it too just didn't dare ask, but this is NCO business. He called that same night and we talked for what seemed like hours, the first hour was tame, but after that it got hot and heavy, we both shared what we wanted while I was here and available. The next day I'd get to see him again in class, don't ask me how, but the dude looked sexier than the day before. I could even smell his cologne every time he walked close by. On our first afternoon break he gave us 20 minutes which was odd, but then he asked for a volunteer to help him pick up some weapons and without even raising my hand I was it. Some looked like they knew what was up, but we knew each other enough to comment. He told me to leave my gear in the classroom and we left. We spoke a bit bout the Army, our jobs, families, just getting a little acquainted, but as soon as we got to the Armory small talk was over, we stepped in, he closed up behind us and had me against the iron door on the same breath. WOW!!! He likes it a bit rough, but was sensual about it. His hands in my hair pulling my head back to give him better access (he is a lot taller), he bit my lips so I would open up to him and I did, but he didn't have to bite, even though I liked it like hell. His hands were all over; my uniform top was off without notice. I was so into that damn kiss, his tongue thrusting in and out as if it was his dick, which I already had in my hand, it felt long and thick, yummy. He was blindly grasping at my clothes as if not being able to wait a minute longer. He left my mouth to nibble on my ear and mouth while at the same time trying to take off my tan t-shirt, as soon as that deed was done, slowly but surely his mouth was on my aching breasts, suckling them as would a baby, but Oh God, he was ALL man. Every time he bit my nipple it was ecstasy; don't know if it was the pain or just that it wasn't supposed to be happening, but if it was even possible I felt my pussy wetter than a few seconds before. Can a person fall in love with someone they almost don't know? I believe so; but not this time, this is not love, just some real strong ass lust.

His hand found the way to the buttons of my uniform pants just as mine had already, I was holding on to that delightful cock, his pre-cum slick on my fingers, we looked into each other's eyes when I brought my fingers to my lips to taste him while holding on to that dick with my other hand, he let his head fall back and let out the sexiest moan I've ever heard from a man. His hand had already reached my swollen, wet pussy, he was caressing her as if she would break but that only lasted till I started gyrating on his hand, then all hell broke loose. He turned me around pushing my pants down to my ankles, shoving me against the wall, didn't even have time to think when I felt the thickness of his head trying to enter my tight cunt, his hand reaching for my clit while he entered me hard and rough. He'd only pumped into me a few times when I felt it coming, rushing like a train without brakes, he kept playing with my clit, pulling on my pussy lips, while biting down on my back, shoulder and neck, that did it, I almost fell if not for him holding and still pushing into against the wall, my legs just gave as my orgasm took over. But he still had a bit more to go; he turned me around and kissed me till my kitty was purring to go again. Took me by the waist and sat me atop a rifle rack, took my breasts into his mouth, sucked on them till they hurt, kept going down, reaching my belly ring playing with that for a few but there was another place he needed to be. When his hot mouth started whispering to my pussy I almost went mad, he really was having a conversation with her, he would tease her by blowing on her or giving her light, inviting kisses, at last he looked up into my eyes and asked if I was ready for a real kiss, I of course said yes, to my amazement he started fucking me with his tongue, Oh My he knows what he's doing, then said she needed that kiss more than my mouth did. (Jajajaja maybe so). He whispered to her to cum for him and as much as I tried to hold back she obeyed him and he rewarded her for that, taking all that sweet juice into his mouth, kissing his way down my thigh till he reached my calves while biting them he said my legs were the most beautiful he'd ever seen and he'd kill to be able to see me in a mini skirt with stiletto heels before I left, I laughed it off since it would probably not happen, but who knows. He stood up and said we had to leave, cause we'd taken too long already, he got us cleaned up. But after we were both fully clothed I got this urge, so I pushed him against the wall and kissed him with all the desire I still felt inside, I broke the kiss and fell to my knees, his eyes were a pool of lust as he watched me slowly take his once again hard dick out of his pants thru his buttons, I smiled and said, "Sorry just have to." I looked up into those sexy bedroom brown eyes and gave him a show; I licked the underside of his thick dick, twirled my tongue around that beautiful head and took him whole into my mouth all the while not breaking eye contact ever. I wasn't even half done when he pulled me by the hair and kissed me roughly, cumming in his hand. Said he didn't want me to have to get cleaned up again, should've seen his face when I said I wouldn't have had to, since I wanted to swallow all of it. What I would have given for a picture of his face at that moment, precious. He swatted my butt on the way out, pulled me against his hard body once outside and whispers in my ear, "This is far from over; before you leave I will have all of you." I had to laugh at that, but didn't really respond anything, because it's been a really long time since ANYONE has had all of me, but I'll have lots of fun letting him believe he can.

Chastity26